MYSTERY OF THE THEATRE GHOST

THE SECRET SEVEN

MYSTERY OF THE THEATRE GHOST

WRITTEN BY PAMELA BUTCHART

ILLUSTRATED BY Tony Ross

For Albie, with all my love. This book was inspired by our first big adventure together.

HODDER CHILDREN'S BOOKS

First published in Great Britain in 2019 by Hodder & Stoughton

1 3 5 7 9 10 8 6 4 2

The Secret Seven®, Enid Blyton® and Enid Blyton's signature are registered trade marks of Hodder & Stoughton Limited
Written by Pamela Butchart. Text © 2019 Hodder & Stoughton Limited
Illustrated by Tony Ross. Illustrations © 2019 Hodder & Stoughton Limited

No trade mark or copyrighted material may be reproduced without the express written permission of the trade mark and copyright owner.

All of the author's moral rights are hereby asserted.

All characters and events in this publication, other than those clearly in the public domain, are fictitious and any resemblance to real persons, living or dead, is purely coincidental.

All rights reserved.
No part of this publication may be reproduced, stored in a retrieval system, or transmitted, in any form or by any means, without the prior permission in writing of the publisher, nor be otherwise circulated in any form of binding or cover other than that in which it is published and without a similar condition including this condition being imposed on the subsequent purchaser.

A CIP catalogue record for this book is available from the British Library.

ISBN 978 1 444 95281 0

Printed and bound in India by Manipal Technologies Limited, Manipal

The paper and board used in this book are made from wood from responsible sources.

Hodder Children's Books
An imprint of Hachette Children's Group
Part of Hodder & Stoughton
Carmelite House
50 Victoria Embankment
London, EC4Y 0DZ

An Hachette UK Company
www.hachette.co.uk
www.hachettechildrens.co.uk

Contents

1	The Travelling Theatre	1
2	The Ghost	6
3	Through the Secret Door	15
4	A Terrible Accident	31
5	The Show Must Go On!	35
6	Opening Night	39
7	Hansel's Dream	46
8	Watch Out!	56
9	Voices in the Walls	62
10	A Quick Escape	70
11	The Rat	74
12	The Terrific Two	81
13	Mystery-Solving Sandwiches	87
14	Ghostly Laughing	99
15	A Midnight Meeting	104

16 The Wig 112
17 A Delicious Picnic 120
18 Who's Gate-Crashing the Picnic? 126
19 The Blackout 135
20 The Ghost Strikes! 139
21 Someone's Locked in the Cupboard! 146
22 Inside the Cupboard 150
23 'A' 157
24 A Blast from the Past 167
25 The Secret Room 174
26 The Return of the Theatre Ghost! 180

[1]

The Travelling Theatre

It was the first Secret Seven meeting of the school holidays and Barbara had some exciting news to share with the other members. As she raced down the garden towards the Secret Seven's shed Peter, the head of the Society, appeared in the doorway, blocking her entrance. 'What's the password?'

'There's no time for that just now. I have some *amazing* news!'

Peter didn't say anything. He just stood there with his arms folded.

'You are so annoying about passwords, Peter. Do you know that?' said Barbara, crossing her arms too and sighing. 'Fine. It's *Scamper.*'

Scamper barked and jumped up, knocking the biscuit Jack had in his hand on to the shed floor. Jack rushed to pick it up before Scamper could get it and shoved it into his mouth.

Colin made a face. 'You didn't even blow on that before you ate it!'

Jack shrugged and kept on chewing.

'I think we need to change the password,' said Janet. 'Scamper gets too excited every time he hears it.'

Just then Pam rushed into the shed to join her friends, shouting, 'SCAMPER! Sorry I'm late.'

Scamper gave a loud bark.

'Don't yell it, Pam!' said Peter. 'It's supposed to be a *secret* password.' He shut the door and took out the official Secret Seven Society notebook. 'Now that everyone's here, let's get started,' he said. 'I think Janet's right about the password. Any suggestions for a new one?'

'*Wait!* First let me tell you my news,' said Barbara. 'They're *here*!' Everyone looked at her blankly and she rolled her eyes. 'The travelling actor people I told you about last week? I saw their van drive past just now. They're on their way to the old theatre in town to set up their show! It's for one week only – and my mum says they're looking for local people to appear as extras in the play. They're holding auditions *today*. Let's go!'

Pam jumped up. 'Can we? I want to go.'

Peter looked annoyed. 'What about the meeting? You just got here and now you want to leave! And you were both *late!*'

'What's the play about?' asked Janet, ignoring her brother. Peter had been in a bad mood all morning and Janet was sure it was because he'd been given the smallest crumpet at breakfast.

'No idea,' said Barbara. 'But I hope it's got *vampires* and *witches* and *werewolves* in it.'

Jack laughed. 'Doubt it! It's probably one of those ones where they all wear big dresses and cry loads. It'll be boring.'

Barbara pointed her finger at Jack. 'I bet it's *not* boring. My mum said that it's a professional theatre company and they usually only go to the big cities.'

'So why are they coming to our village?' asked Jack. 'I didn't even know we *had* a theatre!'

'Exactly!' said Barbara. 'That's why they're coming. That old building with the boarded-up windows in town used to be a theatre. And my mum says that someone's bought it and fixed it up inside and that they've convinced the theatre company to visit our village as part of the grand reopening! I'm definitely going to audition. Anyone else coming?'

Everyone looked at Peter.

'Fine,' said Peter, closing his notebook with a loud THUMP. 'I guess all this important meeting stuff will just have to wait until the next one.'

Janet smiled. She knew that there was no way her brother would let everyone leave if there had been anything really important to tell them. 'Peter, are you coming?' she asked.

'Maybe,' he said, huffily. 'I need to clear up the snacks first.'

'Let me help you with that,' said Jack, stuffing two biscuits into his mouth and putting the rest into his pockets.

Janet grabbed her brother's hand and pulled him towards the door. But then all of a sudden Barbara said, 'Wait. There's something else I should probably tell you.' Barbara's face had gone serious and she wasn't blinking. She put her hand on her chest and took a deep breath.

'Oh, no,' said Pam. 'It's bad, isn't it? What is it, Barbara? Is it your *heart*? Tell us. TELL US!'

Barbara's eyes went even wider. 'Yes, Pam,' she said. 'It's bad. But it's not my heart.'

'Whose heart is it then?' asked Pam.

'It's not anyone's heart,' said Barbara. 'It's a *ghost*.'

[2]

The Ghost

Everyone looked a bit shocked. Except for George. He didn't look like anything because he'd run right out of the shed door the second he'd heard about the ghost.

'I'll go,' said Peter. He was the best at calming George down when he got scared of things like ghosts or cats or Barbara's gran.

'What ghost?' said Colin.

Pam grabbed Janet's hand and gripped tightly.

Barbara took a deep breath. 'OK, so I don't want to worry anyone or anything – and I still really want to go to the theatre and audition to be in the play – but there's a bit of a problem.'

Everyone stared at Barbara.

'After my mum told me about the reopening of the theatre she thought I went upstairs, but I didn't. I went into the kitchen to see if there was any cake left because I was still hungry because we'd had fish for tea and I'd left most of mine because it was a bit too fishy and it had weird black bits on it that Mum said was pepper, but it didn't taste like pepper, it tasted like—'

'BARBARA!' everyone yelled.

'Right. Sorry,' said Barbara. 'So anyway, that's when I heard my mum speaking to my gran about the theatre. She asked my gran how old the theatre is, and my gran said that it's really old and is known to be haunted. Then she told my mum that she'd heard stories about strange noises coming from there at night and that there was no way she was stepping foot inside it because she didn't want to be *haunted*.'

Janet gasped and pulled her hand away from Pam.

'Sorry for squeezing so tight,' said Pam. 'It's just a bit scary!'

Janet smiled. 'It's OK,' she said. She knew Pam got frightened easily. But she didn't give her hand back to Pam in case she squeezed it again.

'Is that it?' asked Jack. 'Is that all she said?

That doesn't mean there's really a ghost! She was probably just trying to be funny!'

Barbara shook her head. 'No. She wasn't. My gran doesn't know *how* to be funny. She's super-serious about everything all the time.'

'She's right,' said George. Everyone turned round to see George in the doorway. 'Barbara's gran is definitely *not* funny. She's terrifying!'

'Are you OK?' asked Janet. 'You look a bit pale.'

'I'm fine,' said George. But no one believed that because his hands were shaking.

'Where's Peter?' asked Janet.

'He's gone to get me a cup of tea from the house,' said George. 'But I don't even need it. I'm fine.'

Janet gave Barbara a look and hoped that Barbara knew that meant she shouldn't say anything else about the ghost just now.

'What's wrong?' said Peter, appearing with a cup of tea for George.

'Nothing,' said Barbara. 'And there's no time for tea.' She took the cup from Peter and placed it down on the desk. 'Auditions start at twelve. Let's go!'

When the Secret Seven arrived at the old theatre they saw other people heading inside for the auditions. Barbara wanted to be first to try out. She threw her bike to the ground and ran in.

'Wait for me!' yelled Pam, running after her.

The rest of the Seven propped their bikes up against the wall of the theatre and looked at George. 'No,' he said. 'I'm not staying with the bikes. I want to audition too.'

Everyone was shocked. George usually *always* wanted to stay with the bikes, especially when they were going somewhere scary. 'I told you before, I'm fine. I'm not even that frightened of ghosts any more. That's not why I ran out of the shed. I . . . er . . . I just needed the toilet, that's all.'

Peter nodded his head, even though he knew George hadn't gone to the toilet. He'd found George sitting under the big tree, taking deep breaths.

'Well, hello there!' said a familiar voice.

Janet turned to see Mrs Bagnell walking towards them with a huge silver case.

Janet smiled. She really liked Mrs Bagnell, who lived in the village and was a friend of the Secret Seven. She used to work in Hollywood making masks and props for horror movies and had even helped them to disguise Pam and Barbara as old women during their last Secret Seven investigation!

Colin rushed to help Mrs Bagnell with her case. 'Wow. That's heavy!' he said.

'It's all my very best stage make-up,' said Mrs Bagnell, proudly. 'It's quite the collection.'

'Are you going to do the make-up for this play?' asked Janet.

'I am,' said Mrs Bagnell. 'I actually used to work with this theatre company a long time ago. They've got their own make-up artist of course, but the poor dear took ill yesterday. So I offered to step in and help out. This grand reopening is all very exciting, isn't it? I love this old place. I worked here for a few months before it closed when I first moved to the village.'

'Do you need any help with the make-up?' asked Janet, excitedly. She'd helped Mrs

Bagnell do the make-up for their school play last year and she'd loved every minute of it.

'I was just about to ask if you'd like to help,' said Mrs Bagnell. 'But are you sure you wouldn't prefer to be onstage? I assume that's why you're all here? Or perhaps you're on official Secret Seven business?'

'No, we're not on official business,' said Janet. 'I'd love to help you with the stage make-up.'

'Wonderful!' said Mrs Bagnell. 'Would anyone else like to help?'

'Will you be making monster masks again?' asked Jack.

Mrs Bagnell laughed. 'No, not this time,' she said.

Jack looked disappointed. 'I knew this was going to be a boring old play in a boring old theatre,' he said.

'Jack!' said Janet. 'Don't be so rude.'

'What?' said Jack. 'I'm just saying that this place looks really dull, that's all. I'd rather be back in the shed getting on with our next adventure.'

Mrs Bagnell raised her eyebrows. 'Oh. You

think so, do you? Well, why don't you follow me and see just how boring this old place is for yourself?'

They all headed up the front steps and inside the theatre. 'Oh, I just love that smell!' said Mrs Bagnell, breathing in the air of the foyer. Janet liked it too. It smelt like popcorn and old wood and it reminded her of Christmas.

'OK, follow me,' said Mrs Bagnell, leading them away from the people who were making their way towards the auditions.

'Um. I think the auditorium is this way, Mrs Bagnell,' said Peter, pointing to a large set of red doors.

'Trust me,' said Mrs Bagnell with a little smile on her face.

So everyone followed her through a narrow door that led to a long, dimly lit corridor.

Jack pointed up at the walls as they passed through. They were covered in old posters. 'Look how old these are,' he said. 'This one's advertising a show starting in July 1925!'

George looked up at the faded poster and swallowed. 'Um, how old is this theatre exactly, Mrs Bagnell?' he asked.

'Oh, I think it's been here since the 1850s,' she said.

George gulped and everyone knew it was because he was thinking about the ghost thing again.

Colin took a deep breath and let it out slowly. The strip light above their heads kept flickering on and off and the corridor seemed to go on for ever. And, even though he was sure he was imagining it, it seemed like it was getting narrower and narrower the further they walked down it.

Peter smiled at George and patted his shoulder. He knew George didn't like the dark.

Eventually Mrs Bagnell stopped. 'It's here somewhere,' she said as she pressed the palms of her hands against the corridor wall. Then all of a sudden there was a loud creak and the wall began to move. 'There we go.'

Colin gasped. 'A secret door! Where does it lead?'

Mrs Bagnell smiled. 'Well, you'll just have to come in and find out. Mind your heads,' she said. And then she ducked down and disappeared into the darkness.

[3]

Through the Secret Door

One by one the children followed Mrs Bagnell until everyone was inside a small, musty-smelling room. Mrs Bagnell switched on a lamp in the corner of the room and they looked around. There were more ancient posters hanging off the walls and piles of old show programmes stacked next to a dirty fireplace that had a vase of dead flowers on its mantelpiece. Mrs Bagnell shut the little door behind them.

Colin set the make-up case down on a dusty dressing table. 'Look!' he said, inspecting the closed door. 'You can't even see that it's a door. There's no handle. It just sort of blends into the wallpaper! It *is* a secret door, isn't it? And that's the normal door that leads backstage, over there!'

'You're quite right,' said Mrs Bagnell. 'This theatre is full of quirky things like that. When it was redecorated all the money must have been spent on the auditorium and the parts of the theatre that are on show to the public – virtually nothing has changed backstage. Anyway, I'm pleased this secret room still exists . . .'

'Is this the dressing room?' asked Pam. 'It's quite small.'

'It's one of them, yes,' said Mrs Bagnell. 'One of the old, forgotten ones.'

The children watched as Mrs Bagnell started fiddling with a switch near the floor. Suddenly the light bulbs surrounding the mirror came on brightly and buzzed loudly. 'Good as new!' said Mrs Bagnell, beaming, as she began to unpack her things. 'They have bigger dressing rooms upstairs, but I like this one. It's got character.'

George couldn't wait any longer. He had to ask. 'Mrs Bagnell, is it haunted here?'

Mrs Bagnell laughed. 'I don't think so,' she said. 'But I'll keep my eye out for you.'

Colin couldn't stop staring at the secret door. 'Can you show me how to open it from the inside?' he asked.

'Hmmm,' said Mrs Bagnell as she began to unpack her things. 'I could. But I don't want you running up and down that corridor. I'm not entirely sure there aren't a few rats out there!' Janet waited for the screaming to start. But it didn't. Then she remembered that Pam and Barbara were already at the audition.

Just then a little bell in the corner began to ring.

George jumped. 'What's that?'

'Calm down, dear. It's just a bell. It's to tell us we're needed upstairs,' said Mrs Bagnell. 'Let's go.'

'I thought no one knew we were here?' asked Janet.

'They don't,' said Mrs Bagnell. 'But every dressing room has one. They're all connected.' The bell rang again, and Mrs Bagnell rushed everyone out of the dressing room through the normal door and up a set of narrow wooden stairs. 'Watch your step!' she yelled from the top. 'There're a few pieces missing.'

Peter looked down. There weren't just a few pieces missing; there was almost a whole step gone!

The staircase led up to another long corridor.

'This place is a maze!' said Colin.

Colin took a notepad out of his pocket and started drawing a map.

Eventually Mrs Bagnell stopped at a large black curtain. 'We're here,' she said with a huge grin on her face. And then she whipped back the curtain and yelled, 'TA-DA!'

'*Wow!*' said Colin. 'Look at that! And that! And *that*.'

The group looked out on to the stage and into the auditorium from the wings. There were lots of people rushing around carrying lights and props and pushing rails of costumes, and some actors were standing among it all rehearsing their lines. The auditorium looked very grand. It was filled with red-velvet seats and gold pillars, and a huge chandelier hung from the ceiling.

Colin began bouncing up and down and pointing at the huge spotlights being hoisted up into the ceiling. 'Do you think they need any help backstage?' he asked, eagerly. 'I'd much rather do that than be in the play.'

'I'm sure they would let you help with a few things,' said Mrs Bagnell. 'I'll ask one of the stagehands now. Wait here. But the rest of you'd better go and join the auditions.' She pointed to the foot of the stage where a small group of people were gathered. 'It looks like they've started!'

Suddenly a voice yelled, 'YOU! STOP RIGHT THERE!'

Janet and the others looked over and realised the voice was directed at Barbara. She was crying.

'What's going on?' asked Peter. 'Why is she crying?'

'Maybe her audition isn't going well,' said Jack.

But then a man with wild, wavy hair and large glasses said, 'You were *outstanding*!'

Barbara stopped crying instantly, smiled and took a bow.

Janet and the others rushed down the little steps and over to the foot of the stage where Pam and Barbara were standing.

'Did you see?' Pam said, excitedly. 'The director loved Barbara's audition!'

'What happened?' asked Jack. 'Is that what you've got to do if you want to be an extra?'

'No,' said Barbara, grinning from ear to ear. '*That's* what you have to do if you want an actual part. I'm in the play! I got a part! A proper part! With lines and everything!'

Barbara grabbed Pam and they started jumping around together and taking turns to roar at each other like lions. Some people gave Pam and Barbara strange looks, but the rest of the Seven just laughed. Roaring at each other when they were excited was one of Pam and Barbara's new things.

'I never knew you could cry on demand!' said Peter.

Barbara stopped roaring and looked at Peter. 'Remember that time you tried to take my Secret Seven badge away because I was late to a meeting?'

Peter's mouth dropped wide open. 'That was *pretend* crying?'

Barbara laughed and began jumping around again with Pam.

'Well, I *should* have taken your badge away for that!' said Peter. 'You weren't just late,

Barbara. You were one hour and fourteen minutes late!'

'Hey! I remember that,' said Jack. 'Peter wouldn't let us touch the cheese pies his mum had made until you got there. They were freezing and they'd gone all crusty by the time you eventually turned up.'

Barbara stopped roaring. 'But you still ate them, didn't you?'

Jack shrugged. 'Would've been a shame to waste them,' he said.

The director clapped his hands loudly and everyone stopped talking. 'Attention! If you've come to audition to be an extra, I need you onstage in fifteen,' he said, wiping his forehead with his sleeve. He looked stressed.

'What do we have to do?' asked Jack.

The director seemed a bit annoyed that Jack had asked a question. 'Just stand and look scared. That's it,' he said, flicking through his script. And then he rushed back over to a man standing onstage holding a horse's head.

Jack burst out laughing. 'George, you'll be great at this!'

Janet looked at the man with the horse's

head. 'What's the play about?' she asked Barbara and Pam, who were still jumping up and down.

'It's *amazing*!' said Barbara, continuing to leap about. 'It's . . . all the fairy tales . . . mixed up . . . together. But they've made it . . . really *creepy*!'

Pam stopped bouncing. 'It'd better not be scary,' she said. 'I don't like scary plays. I went to one with my auntie in London last year and it was *terrifying*!'

'Which play was it?' asked Janet.

'*Oliver Twist*,' said Pam.

'*Oliver Twist* isn't scary!' said Janet.

'Yes it is,' said Pam. 'What about the bit where they wouldn't give Oliver any more food? That's scary. He could have starved to death!'

Everyone burst out laughing.

Pam crossed her arms. 'Stop laughing at me,' she said, giggling too.

'QUIET!' someone shouted from the stage.

They stopped laughing and looked up. There was a woman with long blonde hair dressed as Little Red Riding Hood staring at them. She looked angry. 'Can't you see the *real* actors are trying to rehearse?' The woman turned and glared at the director. 'It was a terrible idea to ask locals to be part of the play! They don't even know how to behave in a theatre. And tomorrow is opening night! What were you thinking?'

The director sighed. 'I've told you before. I want the crowd of villagers to be as *authentic* as possible. Casting locals and giving them as little rehearsal time as possible is part of my *vision*, Finola!'

'I think you should watch your tone with me,' said Finola, sharply. 'I don't *need* to be here, you know. I'm a highly successful shampoo model, in case you'd forgotten! So I suggest you do something about these amateurs. Or I'll *walk*!' And then she stormed offstage.

'Finola!' the director shouted after her. 'We need you onstage! We're just about to rehearse the big scene!'

But Finola was gone. The director looked at an actor wearing a short tunic and tights, who Barbara guessed was playing Rumpelstiltskin.

'Could you *please* try to get her back onstage?' he asked.

Everyone watched as Rumpelstiltskin ran off. The director threw his script to the ground and rubbed his face with both hands.

'Who was *that*?' whispered Janet.

'That's Finola,' said Barbara. 'The lead actress. She's a bit of a nightmare. I hear she threatens to quit the play all the time.'

'How do you know all this?' asked Peter.

'I was chatting to one of the stagehands when I came in,' said Barbara. 'That's how I found out there was a speaking part. She said the director keeps adding extra bits to the play, which really annoys Finola.'

'Finola looks familiar,' said Janet.

Barbara nodded. 'She's a model too. She's on that new shampoo poster up in town.'

Just then Colin appeared. 'So are they going to let you help with those huge lights?' Janet asked.

'No,' said Colin. 'But one of the stagehands said I could help pull the props on and off the stage, which is pretty cool. I have to dress completely in black so the audience can't see me.'

At that moment the director rushed over to the edge of the stage and said, 'You!' The director was pointing his rolled-up script at George. 'That's perfect!' Get up here and show everyone your face.'

George just stood there looking terrified.

'Go on!' hissed Barbara, pushing him up the steps and on to the stage.

The director grabbed George by the shoulders. 'Everyone! *This* is the face you need to make,' he said. '*This* is the face of someone who has just met a giant wolf dressed as an elderly woman!'

Jack was confused. 'What *is* he talking about?' But no one answered. They were too busy watching George. He looked like he was going to faint!

Eventually the director let go of George's shoulders and George wobbled a bit before getting his balance. 'Great work, young man!' the director said, slapping him on the back.

George smiled nervously.

'Um. Did I miss something?' asked Jack.

'Did he just say something about a wolf woman?'

'I think he's talking about the wolf from *Little Red Riding Hood*,' said Peter. 'Barbara says the play's about fairy tales.'

'*Creepy* fairy tales,' said Barbara. 'I told you it wouldn't be boring!'

The director clapped his hands again. 'OK, everyone, listen up. Change of plan,' he said. 'It doesn't look like Finola is coming back any time soon so let's do the audition for the villagers now. Those of you still to try out, up you come!'

Pam and Jack ran on to the stage. 'You coming?' Jack asked, looking down at Peter.

Peter shrugged. He was still feeling a bit annoyed that everyone had abandoned the meeting.

'Suit yourself,' said Jack. 'But you'll be the only one not involved. I thought the Secret Seven were supposed to stick together, you know, in case something happens and we need to act fast?'

Peter thought about that for a moment. 'Fine,' he said, rolling his eyes. 'I'll audition.'

Jack winked at Janet and she winked back. Jack always knew what to say to Peter.

The director watched closely while everyone onstage pretended to be scared. George looked annoyed. 'Are they pretending to be me? I don't look like that!' he grumbled.

'Excellent!' cried the director. 'See you all back here tonight at five for rehearsal. And don't any of you dare to be late!' he said, peering at them over the top of his glasses. 'Now clear off – we're about to rehearse the big scene!' He looked out into the auditorium. 'Where's Rosalind? I need her to step in for Finola.'

'We did it!' squealed Pam as the children jumped down off the stage. 'We're in the play!'

'I can't believe he let whoever was standing at the back be in the show,' said Peter. 'Did you hear them? They were chatting and giggling nonstop.'

Just then Peter felt a tap on his shoulder and he turned to see Jack's annoying little sister, Susie, and her friend Binkie.

'Could you stop talking about us, *please*?' said Susie, grinning.

'What are *you* doing here?' said Jack. 'You never said you were coming!'

Susie crossed her arms. 'It's a free country, isn't it? We came to audition same as you did. And you never told *me* you were coming here either, did you?'

Jack took a deep breath and closed his eyes for a second. 'For the hundredth time I do not have to tell you where I'm going. It's *you* that's supposed to tell *me*. I'm the oldest, remember?'

Susie scowled. 'How is that fair? So what if you're older than me? What's that got to do with anything?'

Jack's face was starting to turn red. His little sister really got on his nerves. 'Because Mum says I'm supposed to keep an eye on you. *That's* what it's got to do with anything.'

'Well,' said Susie, 'there must be something wrong with your eyes then, because you're obviously not doing a very good job if you didn't even know I was here.'

'Yeah!' said Binkie. 'We followed you here.

That's how we found out about the play anyway.'

Susie shot Binkie a look.

'Oh. Sorry, Susie,' said Binkie, looking embarrassed.

'So you've been following us again, have you?' said Peter.

'Nope, we haven't actually,' said Susie, smiling.

Peter narrowed his eyes. 'Yes you have,' Peter said, getting cross. 'Binkie just told us!'

'Wrong again, King Peter,' said Susie. 'We've been following Jack, not you,' she added, walking off.

Peter looked at Jack.

'I know! I know!' said Jack, throwing his hands in the air. 'But she doesn't listen to anything I say. I'll speak to my mum about her again this afternoon.'

'You'd better,' said Peter. 'She can't be following us all over the place and spying on our secret meetings. Some day she's going to completely ruin one of our investigations!'

'Calm down, Peter,' said Janet. 'It's fine. There's nothing for her to overhear, is there?'

Janet didn't like Susie very much, but she knew that Susie couldn't have overheard anything about an investigation at the meeting this morning because there hadn't really been a meeting. And there was nothing to investigate.

'Right, let's get back to the shed and finish our meeting before Susie notices we're gone,' said Peter.

'I need to find Mrs Bagnell first to see what she would like me to help her with,' said Janet.

'And I need to get home and find black clothes for tonight,' said Colin.

Peter looked disappointed. 'Fine. Well, maybe we should just forget about the whole Secret Seven Society since you're all too busy with the play,' he said, and stormed off towards the exit.

But then all of sudden there was a loud, piercing scream from the stage.

[4]

A Terrible Accident

'What was that?' cried George.

Everyone turned and looked up at the stage.

'Is she *dead*?' one of the actors cried.

Peter rushed back over to the foot of the stage. 'What's going on? Is this part of the play?' he asked.

Barbara shook her head. 'I don't think so!'

The Seven raced up the stairs and on to the stage. And that's when they saw the hole.

'SOMEONE CALL AN AMBULANCE! NOW!' yelled the director.

Peter rushed over to help.

'STAY WHERE YOU ARE!' the director shouted at him. 'One of the trapdoors has malfunctioned. There's another one near where you're standing.'

'PETER! DON'T MOVE!' screamed George.

Peter almost jumped out of his skin.

'Thanks, George,' said Peter. 'Did someone fall down there?'

The director's face had gone pale. 'Yes,' he said, looking through the open trapdoor. He lowered his voice, 'She's not moving. Someone get down there, quick!'

Suddenly a young woman with short brown hair appeared from backstage.

'Daniela! Thank goodness!' said the director. 'There's been an accident.'

'I know. I saw from backstage. I've already called the ambulance,' she said. 'Stay where you are. I'll check the other trapdoors are secure and then go down and see how Finola is.'

'It wasn't Finola who fell,' said the director. 'It was Rosalind.'

Daniela's face fell. '*Rosalind?*'

'She had to step in for Finola,' said the director.

Daniela rushed across the stage.

'Be careful,' said Peter.

'It's OK,' she said. 'I'm one of the stagehands. I know exactly where the trapdoors are.'

The Seven watched as Daniela checked the

other trapdoors were secure and then ran down the steps and unlocked a small door at the foot of the stage.

Just then the auditorium doors swung open and paramedics came rushing down the aisle.

'She's in here!' said Daniela, holding the door open for them.

'Is she OK?' the director shouted down.

'She's conscious. But just give us a moment to check her out,' one of the paramedics called back.

'I've no idea how this happened!' said Daniela. 'I checked everything twice before rehearsals started today. Everything was secure, I promise!'

The Seven looked at Daniela. She seemed terrified.

'Don't worry,' said the director. 'It was an accident.'

Just then Finola rushed on to the stage. 'I'm here!' she said. 'We can start the rehearsal now. I got locked in my stupid dressing room.'

Everyone stared at her.

'What?' she asked, touching her head. 'What's wrong. Is it my hair?'

The director pointed to the hole. 'Rosalind fell during the rehearsal,' he said.

Finola's face dropped. 'You let Rosalind play my part and started the rehearsal without me?'

Everyone turned and stared at her again.

'I mean, oh my goodness! Rosalind, are you all right down there?'

They all watched as the paramedics brought Rosalind out on a stretcher. Finola rushed down from the stage and took her hand. 'You poor dear,' she said. 'Are you all right? Do you have any idea what happened? Do you remember anything?'

Rosalind shook her head.

'It looks like her leg might be broken,' said one of the paramedics. 'She's in too much pain to talk right now.'

'Of course,' said Finola, patting Rosalind's hand. 'Off you go. Don't worry about a thing. I don't need an understudy anyway.'

[5]

The Show Must Go On!

When the Secret Seven arrived back at the theatre at five o'clock the director was even more stressed out than he had been earlier. He was pacing up and down, ripping pages from his script and throwing them over the side of the stage.

'Maybe he's a bit worried after what happened to Rosalind,' said Jack. 'I mean, when I go onstage I'm definitely going to avoid standing on a trapdoor!'

'What do you think actually happened?' asked Peter.

'What do you mean?' asked Janet.

Peter looked at the rest of the Seven. 'Do you think it really *was* an accident?'

'Of course!' said Barbara.

'But Daniela said she checked all the trapdoors twice before the rehearsal. She was pretty adamant about it,' said Peter.

Jack laughed. 'Peter, you can't just make up a mystery because you want one! If you want to have a Secret Seven meeting so badly, we can have one first thing tomorrow morning. You bring the snacks!'

Peter rolled his eyes. 'That's not what I'm doing,' he said. 'I'm just pointing out that there doesn't seem to be an explanation for what happened to Rosalind. Trapdoors can't open themselves.'

'These ones probably can!' said Jack. 'I mean, the new owners haven't really fixed anything up backstage, have they? The lock was probably just old and faulty.'

'Or maybe it was a *ghost*!' said Pam. 'Like Barbara's gran said!'

Just then the director threw down what was left of his script and stormed past them.

'What's wrong with him?' Barbara asked one of the actors who was sitting at the side of the stage with her head in her hands.

'More changes,' she said. 'He decided at the last minute that the play wasn't working, so he's added in some new scenes. Everyone's a bit stressed about it. Especially because of the whole food-poisoning thing.'

'What food-poisoning thing?' asked Barbara.

The actress looked up at Barbara. 'We've lost our special-effect guys. *Both* of them! They got sick and had to leave. Food poisoning, we think,' she said. 'The stagehands are going to help with the smoke machine and the lights, but they're not very familiar with our equipment.'

Jack stared at the tea trolley set up at the side of the stage. He'd spotted it as soon as they'd walked in. There were scones and jam next to the tea. And he was sure he could see some clotted cream too.

'Do you know what caused the food poisoning?' he asked. He really hoped it wasn't the scones.

'No idea,' said the actress. 'But I hope I don't get it!'

'I need Gretel onstage!' yelled the director, suddenly reappearing with a giant mug of coffee.

The actress jumped to her feet. 'Better go!'

Peter turned to the others. 'Do you still think there's nothing strange going on?' he asked. 'First the make-up artist gets ill. Then Rosalind falls through a trapdoor and breaks her leg. And now the only two people who know how to do the special effects get food poisoning.'

Jack shrugged. 'OK. So a few strange things have happened, but it could just be coincidence.'

Peter shook his head. 'I don't think so,' he said. 'I think something's up. We need to keep our eyes open.'

[6]

Opening Night

The next day the Secret Seven were all excited about the grand opening. As they cycled to the theatre that afternoon Peter reminded everyone to stay alert and keep an eye out for anything unusual. Even though last night's rehearsal had gone smoothly he was still suspicious. But as soon as they arrived, the Seven were kept busy. Barbara, Pam, Jack and George rushed off for last-minute costume fittings and Janet was doing make-up with Mrs Bagnell. Peter had decided to help Colin backstage with the props, so he and Colin were running through their instructions with the stagehands.

Finally it was time to begin. Barbara, Pam, George and Jack were in the wings with the other actors, waiting for the curtain to go up. They could hear the audience talking and there was excitement in the air. Pam squeezed Barbara's hand and Jack gave George a friendly nudge. The director would be thrilled – George looked more terrified than ever!

The curtains opened, revealing the actors in place, ready to start. But just as the actor playing Daddy Bear started saying his first line the curtains immediately closed again. The audience laughed, especially when one of the three bears got stuck on the wrong side of the curtain and had to crawl underneath to get back.

'Get that curtain up!' hissed the director from backstage.

'We're trying!' said Daniela as she and the other stagehand, Taj, tugged at the ropes. 'There's something wrong with it.'

Eventually Daniela and Taj managed to get the curtain to go up and stay up, and the play began.

After a while everyone started to relax. Things were going smoothly and the children could focus on the action onstage.

'This play's weird,' said Jack. 'Why is Little Red Riding Hood dancing with the gingerbread men?'

Barbara sighed. 'Pay attention, Jack,' she

said. 'Little Red Riding Hood just saved the gingerbread men from being eaten by the wolf and now they're off to a dinner party at the three bears' house.'

Jack shook his head. This play didn't make any sense to him.

'Is anyone else feeling really nervous?' Pam asked.

But no one got a chance to answer because all of a sudden there was a loud screeching sound and everyone's hands went flying up to their ears.

'IS THAT THE FIRE ALARM?' cried George.

Barbara shook her head and pointed to a large speaker.

Just then Taj came running past and pulled on a wire near their feet. The noise stopped.

'What on earth was that?' hissed the director.

'I'm sorry!' said Taj. 'There's a problem with the speaker system. I'll fix it.'

The director looked like he was going to scream. But he didn't. Instead he walked out onstage. 'Ladies and gentlemen,' he said, calmly, 'we are experiencing some slight technical difficulties. The play will commence in just a few moments. Please accept our apologies.'

The children watched as Taj fiddled with the speaker system. 'Someone's been tampering with this,' he said. 'The power cords are all plugged into the wrong sockets!'

Suddenly the music that had been playing before the screeching came through the speakers again and Little Red Riding Hood and the gingerbread men rushed back onstage.

'Can you please get a handle on things?' said the director to Taj. 'Where's Daniela?'

'She's got to stay next to the curtain. It keeps malfunctioning,' Taj said. 'It's not our fault! Someone's been tampering with the speaker wires and I think the curtain has been messed with too.'

'Have you seen my head?' a voice from behind them said.

Jack almost jumped out of his skin. 'Sorry. Your *what*?'

'My *head*!' the actor said. 'I'm due onstage but I can't find my head anywhere!'

It was quite dark backstage, so it took Jack a moment to realise the actor was wearing a furry wolf suit.

'Where did you see it last?' asked Pam.

'*Right there!*' the actor hissed, pointing to a chair. 'Someone must have moved it!'

Just then Finola began talking about the wolf onstage. 'I wonder where that *silly* old wolf is,' she said.

'What am I going to *do*?' hissed the wolf. 'I can't go out there without my *head*!'

'Oh, wooooooolf!' called Finola, a bit angrily, from the stage.

The audience laughed. They'd realised that this wasn't part of the play and that the wolf was supposed to be onstage by now.

'You're just going to have to walk out there and pretend to be a wolf,' said Barbara, firmly. 'Head or no head. You can do it.'

The wolf stared at her.

'*Go!*' said Barbara.

The wolf blinked, turned and then ran out on to the stage.

'Oh. Um . . . Well,' said Little Red Riding Hood when she saw the headless wolf.

The audience began to laugh again.

'Well, at least the audience are enjoying themselves!' said Jack as he pulled a scone filled with jam and cream out of his pocket.

'Where did you get *that* from? I thought they were all eaten yesterday,' said Pam.

'I was too full after my mid-afternoon snack to eat more than a couple,' said Jack. 'So I stuffed a few in my pockets. Should have enough to keep me going for a while.'

'Oh, *yuck*!' said Pam. 'Your pockets will be covered in cream!'

Jack shrugged. 'I'll lick them clean later.'

'You're disgusting,' said Pam.

Jack grinned and then opened his mouth to say something else but shut it again quickly. The others looked at him. He was staring past them.

George turned to see what it was just as a flash of something white flicked round the corner.

'What was that?' asked George.

But Jack just stood there, not answering.

'What's wrong with your face?' said Barbara. 'You look like you've seen a ghost!'

Jack slowly turned his head to face Barbara.

'Oh, no,' said Pam. 'You *did* see a ghost, didn't you?'

'Um . . .' said Jack. 'I think I might have.'

[7]

Hansel's Dream

The curtain had gone down for intermission three full minutes ago, but Pam, George, Barbara and Jack could still hear the audience laughing from the green room.

'It's not supposed to be a funny play!' Barbara complained. 'My part's coming up soon. Nothing better go wrong. I don't want to be laughed at!'

'Did you really see a ghost?' Pam asked Jack.

Jack shrugged. 'It was dark. It could have been anything.'

'What did it look like?' asked George.

'Honestly,' said Jack, 'it looked a bit like a white sheet floating about. But I only saw it for a second before it disappeared round the corner.'

'Excuse me,' said a voice. Jack looked up to see the actress who played Gretel staring at him with wide eyes. 'Are you talking about the ghost?'

Pam gasped. 'Yes!' she said. 'We are! Did you see it too?'

Gretel waved at Hansel to come over. 'Tell them what you saw,' she said.

Hansel plopped himself down next to Pam on the couch and buried his head in his hands. 'I don't know if I can,' he said. 'Every time I tell it it's like I'm reliving it all over again!'

'You don't have to tell us if you don't want to,' said Pam, patting his shoulder.

'No, I want to,' said Hansel, sitting up straight. He seemed much better all of a sudden. 'It all started when I woke up this morning,' he said, rising to his feet as the actors nearby gathered around. 'I'd had an odd dream. *You* were in it!' He pointed to George.

George gulped.

'What about me?' asked Pam. 'Was I in it?'

Hansel nodded his head eagerly. 'All of you were. It was about this theatre. I dreamt that we were performing onstage when a ghost appeared and made us all freezing cold.' He pulled his knees up to his chest and began to rock. 'And then the entire theatre went dark!'

The people around them gasped.

'Now that you've seen the ghost I know that it was a premonition!' said Hansel. And then he slumped back down on to the couch and put his head in his hands again.

'Someone get this man a drink of water!' one of the actors yelled.

'Wait,' said Jack, 'so you didn't actually see a ghost?'

'Yes! I saw it in my dream!' said the actor.

'But I'm not even sure that what I saw was a ghost!' Jack replied.

But no one was listening. They were all too busy fussing over Hansel and trying to get him to take tiny sips of water.

'I think I saw it too!' said one of the other actors.

'And me!' said someone near the back of the group.

'I know all about the theatre ghost,' said Mrs Bagnell loudly from across the room. 'It's haunted this theatre for years!'

Everyone gasped and rushed over to where Mrs Bagnell was sitting.

Suddenly Peter and Colin appeared. 'Come with us,' whispered Peter.

The others stared at him. And then they all burst out laughing.

'Oh, Peter,' said Pam. 'What are you *wearing*?'

'I don't want to talk about it,' he said. But it was hard not to. Because Peter was wearing a pair of women's black tights and a black frilly blouse.

'You all need to come with us right now!' said Peter.

'Ha!' said Jack. 'We're not going anywhere until you tell us why you're dressed like that!'

'Did the director give you a part in the play?' asked George.

Peter sighed and shook his head. 'Look. I was supposed to wear black for going on and off the stage with the props and I completely forgot. This was all they had in the costume room.' Peter made a face and pulled at his tights and everyone burst out laughing again.

'I don't know what you're all laughing at!'

said Peter. 'You don't look much better than I do! Jack's trousers are about five sizes too small for him and George is wearing the weirdest hat I've ever seen in my life!'

George, Pam, Barbara and Jack were dressed up as Victorian peasants. Their clothes were tatty and ripped and Janet had smeared fake mud on their faces.

'We're in *costume*, Peter. We're supposed to look like this,' Barbara said. 'You just look silly!'

'Can we stop talking about my tights for one second?' Peter yelled.

Barbara had to cover her mouth to stop herself from laughing.

Peter rolled his eyes. 'Listen. Colin and I overheard something,' he whispered.

Pam gasped. 'Is it about the ghost?' she asked. 'Jack saw it!'

Peter looked at Jack curiously.

'I saw *something*,' said Jack. 'I never said it was definitely a ghost. It was probably just something white. Part of a costume or a prop.'

'Floating around by itself?' asked Barbara.

Peter checked to make sure no one was

listening to them. 'There's no ghost,' he said, shaking his head.

'You don't know that!' said Barbara. 'Jack isn't the only one who saw it. Some of the actors said they saw it too!'

'I NEVER said I saw it!' said Jack, raising his voice.

'And Hansel even had a dream that the theatre was haunted!' said Pam.

'Oh, well!' said Peter. 'If Hansel had a *dream* about it, then it *must* be true.'

Pam scowled at Peter. She hated it when he made fun of her.

'Mrs Bagnell thinks there's a ghost too,' said George. 'She said she's known about it for years. She probably didn't give me a straight answer when I asked her yesterday because she didn't want to scare me.'

'Listen, I really don't think there's a ghost,' said Peter. 'But there might be a *person*. We found out something suspicious about the trapdoor. But we can't speak here. Follow me.'

Peter led them backstage, along a corridor and down the wooden, winding stairs they'd come up earlier.

'Where are we going?' asked George.

'To get Janet,' said Peter. 'We need to have an emergency Secret Seven meeting.'

Barbara stopped. 'What! Now? We're in the middle of the play!'

Peter gave Barbara one of his this-is-serious faces.

'Fine,' said Barbara. 'But it'd better be quick. My part's next.'

When they arrived at Mrs Bagnell's dressing room a smile spread across Janet's face as she saw what Peter was wearing. But then she noticed how serious he looked. 'What's wrong?' she asked.

Peter peeked into the dressing room. 'Is Mrs Bagnell back yet?' he said. 'We need to have an emergency Secret Seven meeting.'

'No,' said Janet. 'She went upstairs to get some more cotton wool balls as soon as we'd finished the make-up for the first half. But that was ages ago actually. I'm not sure why she's not back yet.'

'Well, she was speaking to some of the actors in the green room. Maybe she's helping them look for the missing head,' said Jack. 'Is there anything to eat in here?'

'What missing head?' asked Janet.

'Haven't you heard what's been happening?' asked Jack.

Janet shook her head. 'I've been down here tidying up. The place was a complete mess after doing Rumpelstiltskin's face. He made Mrs Bagnell change it over and over again, even though it was perfect. He's a nightmare. Why? What's been happening? Is the play going well?'

'Um . . . *NO*!' said Barbara.

'It's chaos up there!' said Jack. 'Everything that could possibly go wrong onstage has gone wrong.'

'We think it's the ghost,' said Pam.

'No we *don't*,' said Peter.

Janet looked at her watch. 'The second half of the play starts in five mins!' she said.

Peter nodded. But it was obvious from the look on his face that he still thought they needed to have a meeting.

'Quick,' said Janet. 'Shut the door and sit down.'

Everyone sat down and looked up at Peter.

'OK,' he said, taking a deep breath, 'just before the performance started, Colin and I overheard the stagehands, Taj and Daniela, talking about the spare trapdoor key. They said it had been missing since yesterday when Rosalind had her accident.'

'They said that the spare key wasn't on the hook next to the fire alarm like it should have been,' said Colin. 'And they sounded worried about it.'

Janet looked at Peter. 'You think someone took it and opened the trapdoor on purpose, don't you?' she said.

'I think it's very suspicious that the key is missing,' he replied. 'I mean, it can't be an accident if neither Taj nor Daniela knows where it is, can it? Maybe someone is behind it all?'

'Well. Either way, I think it's up to the Secret Seven to find that out,' said Colin.

'I agree,' said Janet.

All of a sudden the little bell started to ring.

'Time to go,' said Jack. 'OK, Peter, we'll

keep an eye out for any evidence. The show must go on!'

Everyone except Janet rushed out. She took Peter's arm as he was leaving. 'Be careful,' she whispered. 'If someone did open that trapdoor on purpose, then you might all be in danger up there.'

[8]

Watch Out!

Everything was going fine during the second act. The audience weren't laughing and Barbara's part was coming up soon. Barbara took a deep breath backstage.

'You'll be great,' whispered Pam, squeezing her hand.

Just then they both heard a loud cackle that meant the witch was trying to bake Hansel and Gretel into a pie (which was Barbara's cue to go onstage).

'*Go!*' whispered Pam.

As the witch stirred Hansel and Gretel in a large pot the audience was staring at her, transfixed. Barbara wasn't surprised. Farah, who was playing the part of the witch, was fantastic! Barbara took a deep breath and stepped out on to the stage. 'My dear brother and sister!' she sobbed. 'Please don't eat them! I'll do ANYTHING!'

'Hmmmm,' said the witch. 'Anything, will yoooooou?'

'Oh, yes,' said Barbara, dropping to her knees. 'Anything! Please just let my beloved Hansel and Gretel go.'

'Then tell me a secret. And make it a good one! I eat secrets too, not just children!'

This was it. Barbara's favourite part. She knew her lines inside out and had practised them over and over at home the evening before. She was just going to launch into her monologue, about how she had once stumbled across a house where three talking bears lived and how the littlest one, Albie, had shown her how to make the best porridge in the world and made her promise that she'd never tell a soul the recipe, when she looked up and saw a shadow behind the witch's head.

At first she thought it was the *Little Red Riding Hood* wolf, but he wasn't supposed to eat the witch until the end of her speech. And that's when she realised it wasn't the wolf – it was a tree. And the tree was falling. Fast!

'MOVE! GET OUT OF THE WAY!' yelled Barbara.

But Farah just stood there, staring at her as the tree continued to fall.

Everyone was whispering to each other after the show. Farah had managed to move out of the way at the very last second but it had been close.

'This really is outrageous,' said Finola, pretending to be talking to one of the male actors but speaking loudly so everyone else could hear her. 'Poor, lovely Farah could have been seriously injured. I blame those horrible boys from the village. They shouldn't be allowed to touch the scenery!'

Peter glanced at Colin who looked a bit like he was going to cry.

'Just ignore her,' said Peter. He and Colin hadn't been anywhere near the tree scenery. They'd already been well warned by the stagehands that they shouldn't touch the trees. Now Peter knew why. They were clearly dangerous!

'Everyone, calm down,' said the director. 'It was an accident. It's no one's fault.'

'YES IT IS! It's the stagehands' fault!'

shouted the actor who played Rumpelstiltskin. 'They haven't been trained properly. You there,' he said as Daniela walked past carrying a large piece of gingerbread house. 'Do either of you know what you're doing? Are you even trained?'

'I know exactly what I'm doing!' said Daniela.

'THEN WHY DID THAT TREE ALMOST LAND ON FARAH?' Rumpelstiltskin yelled.

'Taj and I checked all the scenery was locked into place before the performance. Twice! Just like we always do!' she said, beginning to cry.

'Well, that's not good enough, is it?' said the actor.

'Does anyone else think it's strange that all these accidents keep happening?' asked someone else.

Everyone began nodding and whispering to each other. And then one of the actors said, 'Perhaps they're not actually "accidents"! Maybe someone's doing all of this.'

'Everyone, calm down,' said the director. 'Of course they're accidents.'

'But this theatre's haunted,' someone else said. 'What if it's the theatre ghost?'

Then all of a sudden there was a bang from the smoke machine and the theatre began to fill with smoke.

'RUN!' screamed George. 'It's the THEATRE GHOST!'

[9]

Voices in the Walls

'Ok, so I think we can all agree that there's something strange going on at the theatre,' said Peter as soon as he shut the shed door the next morning.

Peter had told everyone to be at the shed for 11 a.m. *sharp*, and everyone had turned up on time, even Pam and Barbara.

'We know!' said Pam. 'It's a *haunting*!'

'Maybe it's a curse!' said Barbara.

'I thought you said it was a ghost?' said Jack, spreading an extra-thick layer of apricot jam on to a crumpet.

Peter sat down and began rubbing his temples.

'I did. I mean, I do think that! It could be both!' said Barbara. 'A ghost might have cursed the theatre because a long time ago they used to work there or something and—'

'OK,' said Peter, standing up, 'if you're not

going to take this seriously and listen to what I have to say, then this meeting is officially over!'

'Oh, calm down,' said Jack. 'What's wrong with you?'

'Nothing's wrong with me,' said Peter. 'I just want to have a meeting about what's going on at the theatre without it having to be all about ghosts and goblins!'

'I never said a word about goblins,' said Barbara. 'Goblins don't exist.'

Janet tried not to laugh because Peter's head looked like it was going to explode.

'But, Peter,' said George, 'even Mrs Bagnell said there *was* a theatre ghost.'

Peter's right eye started twitching uncontrollably.

'OK, Peter,' said Janet, 'we're listening. Go on.'

'I've called this meeting of the Secret Seven because, like I said yesterday, I think all the stuff that's going wrong at the theatre might be going wrong on purpose,' said Peter. 'I think it might be *sabotage*.'

Barbara opened her mouth to speak but

Peter held up his hand. 'And before you say it, I don't think it's a ghost sabotaging the play,' he said. 'I think it's a human, living person.'

Pam gasped. 'But who would do that?' she said. 'I mean, Rosalind could have broken more than her leg. She could have been killed!'

Peter nodded. 'And Farah could have been seriously hurt when the tree fell onstage, so we need to be very careful. Because if this *is* sabotage, the culprit is obviously dangerous.'

George gulped.

'Do you really think someone is out to ruin the play?' asked Janet.

Peter nodded. 'At first I wasn't sure. But then when I found out the trapdoor key was missing I started to get a bit suspicious. And when scenery almost landed on Farah I knew something was wrong. And then the smoke machine exploded!'

Janet stood up. 'I think Peter's right,' she said. 'It can't just be bad luck that all these things are happening. It does seem like there might be someone out to destroy the play. And if there is, we need to find out who it is before they hurt someone else.'

'If you're right,' said Colin, 'then the person who stole the key is probably behind everything else too. Find the key, find the culprit. We should organise a full search of the dressing rooms and everyone's personal belongings.'

'How are we going to do that without getting caught?' asked Pam.

'Peter and I can search while the actors are onstage,' said Colin. 'We have to wear black and sneak around moving stuff anyway. It's perfect!'

George gulped again. 'That sounds risky,' he said. 'And should we even be going back to the theatre after what happened last night? I mean, it's not very safe, is it? What if something else explodes?'

Peter put his hand on George's shoulder. 'I'm not going to lie to you,' he said, 'we probably shouldn't go. And it *isn't* safe. But if someone is out to sabotage the play, we can't let them get away with it, can we? We're the Secret Seven after all!'

George nodded and took a deep breath. 'You're right,' he said. 'But can we take Scamper? For protection?'

Scamper jumped up from his spot in the corner of the shed and barked loudly.

'Definitely!' said Peter.

As soon as they arrived at the theatre, Janet took Scamper's lead and rushed him over to the narrow door they'd gone through with Mrs Bagnell. They weren't sure if dogs were allowed inside, but they thought it best not to ask in case the answer was no.

Colin gasped. 'Mrs Bagnell showed you how to open the secret door, didn't she?'

'No,' said Janet. 'But I'll figure it out. I'm sure she won't mind when I tell her it's for official Secret Seven business.'

'Oh!' said Barbara, grabbing Pam's hand. 'We'll come with you! We're dying to see the secret passageway!'

'Wait,' said Colin. 'You can't say anything to Mrs Bagnell.'

'Mrs Bagnell already knows we're a Secret Society,' said Janet. 'We can trust her. She won't say a word.'

'No,' said Colin. 'It's not that. It's just we haven't ruled anyone out yet. Everyone in the theatre is still technically a suspect. She can't know we suspect anything.'

'Mrs Bagnell isn't a suspect!' said Janet. 'She's our friend!'

'Fine,' said Peter. 'Just be sure not to tell her any of the details, OK? It's only the seven of us who are allowed to know official Secret Seven stuff.'

Janet nodded and disappeared through the narrow door with Scamper, and Pam and Barbara hurried in behind them.

'It's a bit creepy in here,' said Pam as they made their way along the dimly lit corridor. Suddenly Scamper growled.

'Quiet, boy,' whispered Janet. 'You're OK.'

Janet thought that Scamper must have seen a rat, but she didn't say anything to Pam and Barbara because they didn't know about the rats yet (and she knew that if they did, they'd make a *lot* more noise than Scamper!).

Scamper walked towards Barbara and began sniffing at the wall where she was standing.

'Does anyone else hear that?' said Barbara.

Janet and Pam listened closely.

'Listen,' said Barbara. 'Scamper hears it too.

It sounds like a voice coming from the other side of the wall.'

Just then the noise got much louder and they could clearly hear shouting voices.

Barbara put her ear to the wall and her eyes went wide. 'Someone's speaking about the trapdoor!'

Janet and Pam rushed over and put their ears against the wall as well.

'Oh, yuck, yuck, yuck!' said Pam. 'I think I just leant against a cobweb!'

'Shhhh!' whispered Janet. 'If we can hear them, they might be able to hear us.'

And that's when they all heard a voice say, 'Rosalind deserved exactly what she got. She's been trying to steal my leading role since day one! And can you believe that utterly useless director suggested cutting some of my scenes to make more time for Farah's scenes? Well, he'll soon regret the way he's treated me. They all will!'

Pam gasped and stared at Janet, and Janet stared back.

Then another muffled voice said, 'You're a million times more talented than Rosalind.

And that witch Farah! You're the only star of this show. They'd be *nothing* without you. Don't worry, darling. Soon they'll all be sorry they didn't appreciate you more.'

Scamper started to growl and scratch at the wall. And one of the voices said, 'What was that?'

So they ran.

[10]

A Quick Escape

'Please hurry up!' said Pam.

'I'm trying!' said Janet. 'I can't find it!'

Janet was lost. She thought she'd remember where the secret door that led to the dressing room was, but she didn't. The walls all looked the same and she couldn't see any cracks or gaps or anything that seemed like it might be a secret door. But then she recognised a poster she'd seen near the door. 'I think this is it,' she said, reaching down and pressing the wall with both hands.

Pam and Barbara watched as the secret door opened with a creak and light from the dressing room poured out into the corridor. Once they were all safely inside Pam had to lie down on the floor and pet Scamper for a few minutes until her heart went back to normal. 'I was so scared they were going to catch us,' she said, cuddling into Scamper.

Scamper sniffed Pam's face and gave it a lick.

'They obviously heard him scratching,' said Janet. 'But they probably wouldn't have known where it was coming from. I think it's only Mrs Bagnell who knows about the corridor.'

'I hope so!' said Pam, staring at the spot on the wall that they'd come through. 'Are you sure that's locked?'

'I don't think it *can* be locked,' said Janet. 'You just push it and it pops open and shut.'

'I can't believe she did that to Rosalind,' said Barbara.

Janet stopped and turned to face her. 'You recognised the voice?' she asked.

Barbara looked at Janet and then at Pam. 'Yes,' she said. 'Didn't you?'

Janet and Pam shook their heads.

'I'm not sure about the second voice,' said Barbara. 'But isn't it obvious who said the stuff about Rosalind deserving what happened to her? It was Finola. She said that Rosalind had been trying to steal her leading role!'

Pam gasped and sat up straight. 'Does this mean Finola opened the trapdoor on purpose?' she said.

'That's what it sounded like!' said Barbara. 'She said Rosalind got exactly what she deserved.'

'And Finola wasn't onstage when it happened,' said Janet. 'She had that argument with the director and stormed off in a huff a while before.'

Barbara's eyes went wide.

'What is it?' said Pam. 'What's wrong?'

'Do you remember what she said about getting locked in her dressing room? I bet that was a lie. She was probably hiding under the stage the whole time, waiting to open the trapdoor at the right moment!'

That's when Janet thought of something else. 'And remember what Finola said to Rosalind when she found out she'd broken her leg?' she asked.

Pam and Barbara shook their heads.

'She didn't ask her if she was OK or if there was anything she could do for her,' said Janet. 'She asked if Rosalind had any memory of what happened to her.'

Barbara and Pam gasped at the same time.

'She was worried Rosalind knew it was her!' exclaimed Pam.

Janet nodded. 'She was checking to make sure Rosalind hadn't spotted her down there when she fell,' she said. 'And there's something else.' Pam and Barbara leant in close. 'That wasn't actually the last thing Finola said to Rosalind before she was taken away. The very last thing she said was, "I don't need an understudy anyway."'

Pam gasped.

'You two'd better get upstairs and tell the others what we heard,' said Janet. 'This is getting serious.'

[11]

The Rat

'Are you ready for this?' Peter whispered to Colin.

Colin nodded.

Pam and Barbara had told the others about Finola as soon as they could, and during the intermission the Secret Seven had come up with a plan.

The plan was to wait until Finola went onstage, then Peter and Colin would sneak along the corridor into her dressing room to search for the missing trapdoor key.

Barbara had wanted to go and tell the police right away, but Colin had said that they needed to find *hard evidence* first, because without it they couldn't prove it was Finola. Colin said that if they found the trapdoor key in her dressing room, that would be evidence and then they could let the police know.

Colin and Peter hid in the shadows backstage until they heard their cue.

'Why, I'm Little Red Riding Hood!' Finola said onstage. 'And I'm looking for my grandma.'

Peter nodded at Colin, and Colin looked at his watch and nodded back. They had exactly seven minutes to get into Finola's dressing room, search and get out before she got eaten by the wolf.

Colin held his breath as they sneaked along the corridor and into the dressing room. Peter shut the door behind them.

'This place is huge!' said Colin. 'The search is going to take much longer than we planned!' He was panicking a bit. He didn't know where to start. But he knew that they had to find the key.

'It's OK. Calm down,' said Peter. 'Look. You take this side of the room and I'll do that side, OK? Go!'

'There's just so much stuff in here,' complained Colin as he searched through one of the three wardrobes. 'It could be anywhere!'

'Hold on. What's this?' said Peter, picking something out of the bin. It was a handwritten note that said:

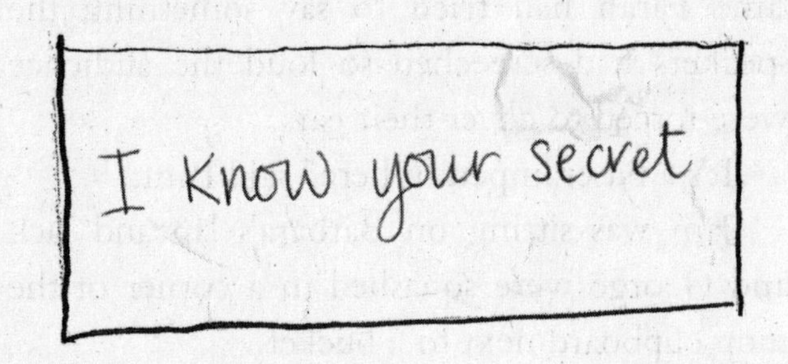

'Do you think someone else suspects Finola too?' asked Peter. 'Maybe someone saw her steal the key. Maybe there's an actual witness!'

Colin took the piece of paper and turned it around in his hands. There was nothing written on the back. It was just those words. 'This could mean anything,' he said. 'We need to find out who wrote it and what the secret is.'

Peter had no idea how they were going to be able to do that. But Colin did.

As soon as the play was finished, Peter called an emergency meeting.

'Well, *that* was a disaster!' said Jack.

And it had been. The first half of the play had been fine, but during the second half every time Farah had tried to say something the speakers had screeched so loud the audience were forced to cover their ears.

'It's a bit cramped in here,' said Pam.

Pam was sitting on Barbara's lap and Jack and George were squashed in a corner of the mop cupboard next to a bucket.

'Are we even allowed to have a meeting without Janet?' asked Barbara.

'We didn't have a choice,' said Peter. 'I just went to get her, but she was busy helping Rumpelstiltskin take off his fake nose. Looks like she'll be in there for a while. It was stuck tight!'

'Did you find the trapdoor key?' asked George.

Peter shook his head. 'But we did find something,' he said, nodding towards Colin.

Colin carefully took the note out of his pocket and held it up to show everyone.

'Can't see a thing,' said Jack. 'Is there a light in here? Do mop cupboards even have lights?'

Barbara pulled on a piece of string near the door and a dim light came on above their heads. 'Oh, yuck,' said Barbara. 'This place is filthy!'

'What's *that*?' squealed Pam, pointing to a corner.

Peter turned and looked at the furry thing which was half hidden behind the bucket and Jack's feet. 'That's a prop,' he said, confidently. 'There are loads of those backstage.'

Peter knew quite well that it wasn't a prop and was actually a rat. He just hoped that the rat was either dead or that it would stay still long enough for them to finish the meeting without Pam and Barbara screaming their heads off. Peter nodded to Colin, who held up the note again. 'We found this in the bin in Finola's dressing room,' said Peter. 'I think it might mean someone saw Finola taking the key or opening the trapdoor.'

'But we don't know that for sure,' Colin added. 'It might be. But it also might be a threat. Or she could even have written it herself. We just don't know. But it *is* suspicious and we need to find out who wrote it. And I think I know how we can do that.'

'How?' asked Jack.

Colin carefully put the note back into his pocket and then he smiled and said, 'Handwriting analysis. We're going to collect samples of everyone's handwriting and then I'll analyse them against the note. I've got a book about it at home.'

'Wait,' said Barbara. 'If Peter's right and someone saw Finola steal the key or open the trapdoor, why would they write her an anonymous note? Why not just tell someone what they saw?'

'Sometimes witnesses are too scared to come forward,' said Colin. 'They might be trying to get Finola to confess herself.'

Barbara thought about that for a moment. Finola *was* pretty scary.

'Oh!' said Pam. 'Or maybe they're scared no one will believe them and that Finola might come after them too!'

'Or maybe you've got it all wrong!' said a voice from behind the door.

[12]

The Terrific Two

Everyone froze.

'It's her!' hissed Pam. 'It's *Finola*!'

Colin looked at Peter. 'Janet?' he asked.

Peter shook his head. He wasn't sure who was on the other side of the door, but he knew it wasn't Janet's voice they'd heard.

But Jack knew exactly who the voice belonged to. The others watched as he rushed forward, knocking the mop and bucket over, and flung open the door. 'I KNEW IT WAS YOU!' he yelled.

Jack's sister Susie was standing there with her arms folded and a huge grin across her face. 'I think you need to seriously consider renaming yourselves,' she said. 'Maybe the *Sloppy* Seven would suit you better, hmm? After all, you're not very good at the whole *Secret* part, are you?'

'Go away,' said Peter. 'We don't have time for this.'

'Nope,' said Susie. 'I want in.'

Peter laughed out loud. 'Never!' he said.

Susie grinned. 'You sure about that, King Peter? Because I now know everything that *you* know about the trapdoor. You think Finola opened it on purpose. And that there's a note from a witness.'

'Well,' said Colin, stepping forward, 'that's not technically true. We don't have enough evidence yet to be sure what "I know your secret" means. We need to find out who wrote the note and—'

'*Shhhhhhh!*' said Jack. 'You just told her what the note said! She didn't know that!'

Susie leant against the doorway, grinning.

'Thanks, Colin,' she said. 'Hey! Maybe you'd like to be in *my* secret society? What do you say?'

Peter almost choked on his own tongue. 'What secret society?'

'Well, since you won't let me join the Sloppy Seven, and because I'm clearly a million times better at solving mysteries than you lot, I think

I should start my own secret society. In fact, yes. I just have. It's me and Binkie. We're called the Terrific Two. And we're *definitely* going to solve this mystery before you!' Before anyone could reply, Susie turned and stormed off.

'Thank goodness!' said Mrs Bagnell, collapsing into the chair as soon as the last person needing their make-up removed had left the dressing room.

'I'll tidy up,' said Janet. 'You take a break.'

'Thank you, dear,' said Mrs Bagnell.

Scamper was curled up fast asleep under the dressing table.

'That Finola. Well! She's a piece of work, isn't she?'

Janet so badly wanted to tell Mrs Bagnell what they'd heard Finola say through the wall and about what they suspected she'd done. But she knew she couldn't. 'She doesn't seem very nice,' she said instead.

'No, she's certainly not,' said Mrs Bagnell, firmly. 'And a few of the others are hard work too! I know some of them from when I used to work with the company in London about ten years ago. There's a new director and a few new faces, but a lot of the original cast have stayed on.'

Janet knew this was a chance to find out more about Finola. 'Did you know Finola back then?' she asked as she started gathering up make-up that was scattered everywhere.

'Yes, actually. She was a child actor when I first met her. Only eleven years old.'

Janet watched as Mrs Bagnell's face changed. She was clenching her jaw.

'I never did like her,' she said. 'Even as a girl she was sneaky and unkind. She was one of the reasons I parted ways with the company.'

'What happened?' asked Janet.

'Oh, it was all such a long time ago,' said Mrs Bagnell, getting up from her chair. 'Shall I help you with the tidying up?'

'No, it's OK, I can manage,' said Janet. She was desperate to hear the rest of the story. 'Did something happen with Finola back then?'

Mrs Bagnell sat back down. 'Yes,' she said, letting out a deep breath. 'We had two child actors at that time. Finola and Adaline. They were the best of friends. Adaline was a beautiful, kind little girl. I was very fond of her. She had long red hair and green eyes, and she was a wonderful actress. The director at the time cast her in the lead child role and it was clear to me that Finola wasn't happy about it.

'And then on opening night Adaline broke out in a nasty rash and had to be taken to hospital. I went to visit her as soon as the play was over and she claimed that Finola had given her a piece of cake she knew Adaline was allergic to. Adaline said Finola told her it had been made without eggs, but it hadn't. I asked Finola about it the next day, but she insisted she'd told Adaline *not* to eat the cake. But I never believed that. Why would Adaline lie?

'So anyway, Finola played the lead role in place of Adaline on opening night and was given rave reviews, and when Adaline returned a few days later the company wouldn't give her the role back. I remember she was so upset, the poor thing. And it didn't help that no one believed that Finola had stolen her part on purpose. I tried to convince Adaline to stay with us and that things would get better, but she left to join another company, which was probably for the best.'

'That's terrible!' said Janet.

Mrs Bagnell nodded. 'The whole thing didn't sit well with me. I tried talking to the director and the rest of the cast, but they didn't want to hear it. The only thing they cared about was good reviews! I left a short while afterwards.'

Mrs Bagnell shook her head as if she was shaking away the memory. By the time she had finished speaking Janet had tidied everything away neatly. 'Right,' Mrs Bagnell said. 'That should be us finished for the night. I'll see you tomorrow then.'

After she left Janet took out the official Secret Seven notebook and wrote down the story Mrs Bagnell had just told her about Adaline.

[13]

Mystery-Solving Sandwiches

Before heading home that night the Secret Seven made a final trip to the green room to put their plan in action.

'Remember to write your name next to your sandwich order,' said Peter as he handed his pad and pen to an actress who played one of the dancing gingerbread men.

'I assume you have fresh-baked wholemeal with poppy seeds?' she asked.

Peter had no idea what that was, but he was sure his mum would have some. 'Of course,' he said.

Janet stared at Peter. She had no idea what he was up to.

'Where's Scamper?' asked Peter.

'I left him downstairs so I could quickly come up and find out about the dressing-room search,' Janet whispered. 'And I have something to tell you.'

'Here! Boy!' yelled Rumpelstiltskin from across the room. 'Come and take my lunch order.'

'I'll go,' said Colin.

'Peter, what's happening?' said Janet.

Peter took Janet to the side and told her about the note they'd found. Janet looked a little upset. Peter made sure Susie wasn't spying on them again and then he said, 'Look, I'm sorry we had a meeting without you, but it was an emergency. I'll explain everything when we get home, I promise. And you can tell me whatever you need to tell me then. But I need to keep asking people to write down what they want in their sandwich for lunch tomorrow so Colin can analyse everyone's handwriting.'

'Peter,' said Janet, looking at the long list of food on Peter's pad. 'Please tell me you're not making sandwiches for the entire cast,' she said. 'Because that's what it looks like!'

'No. Don't be silly,' said Peter. 'I'm going to get Mum to do it.'

'Peter!' said Peter and Janet's mum. 'I don't even know what half of the things on this list *are*!'

'It's just sandwiches, Mum,' said Peter.

Peter's mum gave him a look that could kill. 'Just sandwiches, is it?' Well, could you please tell me where I'm supposed to find *enoki mushroom tapenade*? I don't even know what that is!'

'I'm sure you'll figure it out, Mum,' said Peter, giving her a kiss on the cheek. 'You're the best cook ever.'

Janet shook her head at him. Peter was such a suck-up at times. 'We'll help,' she said.

Peter shot Janet a look. 'We can't,' he said, pointing at the kitchen clock. 'It's already eleven!'

'It's fine,' said their mum. 'Off you go, the two of you.'

Peter opened his mouth to ask about snacks for their meeting, but Janet pulled him out of the kitchen and down to the shed before he could say a word. When they got there everyone was already inside.

'You're a bit late, aren't you?' said Barbara, tapping her watch.

'What's the password, Peter?' said Jack, smiling.

Peter gave them both a look and said, 'Scamper,' before taking his seat. He hated being the last one to the meeting. It was *his* club, after all!

'OK,' said Janet, taking charge, 'I found out something about Finola last night that I think you're all going to find very interesting.'

Everyone listened closely as Janet told them the story of Finola and Adaline.

As soon as Janet was finished, Pam did the loudest (and longest!) gasp that any of them had ever heard. 'She sabotaged her best friend!' said Pam.

Janet nodded. 'And now she's doing it again,' she said. 'Finola got rid of Rosalind because she was worried Rosalind was going to steal her part. And she tampered with the scenery so that the tree would fall on Farah.'

'But why would she do all the stuff like bringing the curtain down at the wrong time and hiding the wolf head and making the smoke machine explode?' asked Barbara.

'I think she's trying to make the director quit or get fired,' said Janet. 'She obviously doesn't like him. And we heard her say that she was going to make him pay for the way he was treating her.'

'But we still can't prove any of this!' said Colin. 'We need something we can actually take to the police.'

'We need to find out who wrote that note, which should be easier than tracking down the missing key,' said Peter. 'Although lots of people didn't put their names next to their sandwich order, so we don't know whose writing is whose. We'll have to remember to ask for everyone's names when we give out the sandwiches today. Mum's making them now.'

'Speaking of sandwiches . . .' said Jack, pointing to his stomach and smiling.

'No snacks today, I'm afraid,' said Peter. 'Mum's too busy making lunch for the cast and crew. And she's only got half an hour to do it because we need to be there for twelve to hand out the sandwiches. And we have to talk about your sister's new secret society before we go!'

'What do you mean there are no snacks?' said Jack. He looked a bit like he was going to cry. 'I've not had any breakfast!'

Janet looked at Peter. 'Did you tell Mum that?'

'What?' asked Peter. 'About Susie's new club?'

'No,' said Janet, 'that she only has thirty minutes to make thirty sandwiches?'

Peter shook his head.

Janet sighed and stood up. 'Right, everyone, up you get,' she said.

'Where are you going?' asked Peter.

'We're going to help Mum,' said Janet.

'*Yes!*' said Jack, and then he rushed out of the door and all the way up to the farmhouse kitchen.

'But what about the meeting?' Peter called after him.

'Don't worry,' said Janet. 'Susie was just trying to wind you up. You know what she's like. She's probably forgotten all about the Terrific Two by now anyway.'

'She'd better have!' said Peter. 'This is an official Secret Seven investigation. I don't need Susie and Binkie coming along and messing everything up.'

'She won't. Now let's go,' she said, pushing her brother out of the shed.

Peter and Janet's mum was in a bit of a state when the Seven got up to the farmhouse. 'What happened?' said Peter. He'd never seen the kitchen so messy!

'Don't worry, we're here to help,' said Jack, eyeing up a particularly tasty-looking cheese and pickle sandwich.

'Thank goodness,' said Peter and Janet's mum, wiping pickle from her forehead. 'Wrap these finished sandwiches and put them in that basket over there, will you? And could you tidy up a little bit while I finish the rest?'

'We'll help you make the sandwiches,' said Janet, nudging Peter. She thought it best just to help get everything finished quickly rather than tell her mum she only had twenty-five minutes left to do it all.

'I'm afraid I've had to cut some corners, Peter,' his mum said. 'Someone asked for smoked salmon with capers on a poppy-seed bagel. So I've made them a tuna sandwich. I hope that's OK!'

Janet had never seen her mum look so

stressed! 'I'm sure it'll be fine,' she said, giving her mum's arm a squeeze. 'Thanks for doing this for us.'

'Well! I wasn't given much of a choice, was I?'

'What's that smell?' asked Colin.

Something smelt delicious.

'Is it the tuna mayo?' asked Peter and Janet's mum. 'I made it fresh today and put some cucumber and dill in it. Thought I'd better. These actors seem a fussy bunch!'

'No,' said Jack. 'It smells like caramel or something.' He was getting excited.

'Oh!' said Peter and Janet's mum. 'I completely forgot. I made a treat for you to take to the theatre. That was before I was told I was catering for thirty people!'

Jack waited patiently as Peter and Janet's mum continued to make a sandwich. He watched as she cut the sandwich in two and handed it to George to be wrapped. And then she picked up more bread and started to make another sandwich. Jack was getting worried that she'd forgotten about the treat again. He waited for as long as he possibly could (which was about seven seconds). 'Did you say you made us a treat?' he asked.

Peter and Janet's mum laughed and put down the butter knife. 'You!' she said, pointing at Jack. 'Come and help finish this ridiculous lunch list while I go and get it.'

Jack practically leapt over the kitchen table. 'What am I supposed to make?'

Barbara pointed to the next sandwich on the list: goat's cheese and caramelised onion on a freshly baked French baguette.

Jack looked at her. 'Cheese roll?'

Barbara nodded, then looked down. 'Poor Scamper,' she said. He was sitting at her feet, watching her every move. 'He's hoping I'll accidently drop something. Aren't you, boy?' Scamper barked loudly.

'Here we go,' said Peter and Janet's mum. 'It took me most of yesterday afternoon to bake this. It's a bit of an invention, I suppose!'

Jack gasped as she plopped a huge cake down on the kitchen table.

Everyone stared at the cake. It was magnificent!

'What kind is it?' asked Pam.

'Well,' said Peter and Janet's mum, 'like I said, it's a bit of an invention! I made too much Scottish tablet, so I thought I'd better come up with a use for it. It's a sponge cake filled with tablet-flavoured cream and covered in fudge sauce and little chunks of tablet. If I had to give it a name, I'd probably call it a Scottish Tablet Surprise Cake.'

'What's the surprise?' asked Jack. His mouth was filling with saliva.

Peter and Janet's mum smiled. 'I've hidden big chunks of tablet inside the cake. It's probably the sweetest cake I've ever made!'

It was the most amazing thing Jack had ever seen.

Scamper barked again and tried to jump up on to the table.

'No!' cried Jack.

'Down, Scamper,' said Peter and Janet's mum. 'Here,' she added, taking a box out of the kitchen cupboard, 'a freshly baked dog biscuit just for you.'

Scamper took the biscuit over to his bed next to the stove in the corner of the kitchen and hid it under a cushion.

'The little devil!' said Janet. 'He's hiding that one for later. He'll walk back over here demanding another one in a second. Just watch.'

And right enough, a moment later Scamper wandered back over and put his paw up on her mum's knee.

'Did you really bake Scamper's biscuits?' asked Jack.

'No,' said Peter and Janet's mum. 'But I do sometimes pop them in the oven for a minute so they're nice and tasty, don't I, boy?'

'Can I give him another one?' asked Jack.

'Well, I suppose so,' she said.

Jack reached over and gave Scamper another dog biscuit. He watched Scamper take it back over to his bed and lie down to eat. Jack let out a sigh of relief. The further Scamper was from the most delicious-looking cake he'd ever seen in his life the better!

[14]

Ghostly Laughing

'Who ordered the chicken and smoked Cheddar panini with extra onions?' cried Jack.

'This is a nightmare,' muttered Peter. 'How are we going to get everyone's names in this chaos?'

'ME! I'm extra onions!' someone yelled from the back of the room.

Jack looked down at the turkey and cheese sandwich in his hand. He was pretty sure 'extra onions' was going to be disappointed.

'Remember to get their name and write it down next to their order,' Peter told Jack.

'What if they won't tell me their name?' asked Jack.

'Then you can tell them I said *no name, no sandwich*! That's the rule! Who's that Barbara just gave a roll to? Did you see her write anything down? I didn't! I have to go,' said Peter, panicked.

'Wow,' said Jack. 'He needs to calm down a bit! Do you really think I should say *no name, no sandwich*?'

Janet laughed. 'No. Definitely not!' she said. 'I think that might make us look a bit suspicious. If you don't know the person's name, just try to ask them casually, OK?'

Jack nodded. 'All this talk of sandwiches is making me hungry. Lucky, I've still got my secret stash of scones with cream,' he said, tapping his pocket before stuffing one into his mouth as he walked off to find 'extra onions'.

Janet rolled her eyes.

'Look over there,' whispered Pam.

Janet followed Pam's gaze until she spotted Finola. She was standing at the back of the room staring at everyone, nervously fidgeting with her hair.

'Do you think she's worried about the note she got?' asked Pam.

Janet nodded. 'That's nervous behaviour, right?' she asked Colin. 'It's in one of your books about interviewing suspects, isn't it?'

'Yes,' said Colin. 'Excessive touching of the

hair and face is very suspicious suspect behaviour.'

Just then Peter came rushing over. 'How are we getting on, Colin?' he asked.

'Well,' said Colin, looking at his list, 'we've almost got everyone's names. And most of them seem happy with their lunch too!'

Janet smiled. Her mum would be pleased when she told her. They might not have been the fancy sandwiches they thought they were getting but she'd known that they would like them. Peter was right. Their mum really was the best cook ever. And everyone was raving about the Scottish Tablet Surprise Cake!

Janet was just about to go and help Pam, because she looked like she was getting a hard time from someone shaking a sandwich at her and yelling something about 'poppy seeds', when she saw a group of actors huddled by the tea trolley.

Janet watched carefully. They were whispering about something. She moved closer so she could hear and that's when she realised they were talking about ghosts!

'I've never seen so many things go wrong

during one production,' said the actress who played Gretel. 'I think what she told us is right. This is the work of a ghost!'

'Me too,' said Hansel. 'I felt something staring at me when I was in the toilet. I had to leave and use the ladies' room instead!'

'And I heard weird scratching and growling noises when I was in my dressing room,' said Rumpelstiltskin. 'It was like there was a ghost trapped in the wall trying to get out!'

Janet knew that it had been Scamper that Rumpelstiltskin had heard. And now she knew that Rumpelstiltskin had been the person they'd overheard speaking to Finola!

Janet took out the Secret Seven notebook and wrote down:

Rumpelstiltskin is second voice (and Finola's partner in crime)

'I knew the minute my head went missing that someone or *something* was up to no good,' someone else whispered.

It took Janet a minute to realise it was the actor who played the wolf who was talking (which made her feel a lot better about the whole missing head thing).

Suddenly the group stopped whispering. Janet thought that it might have been because they'd noticed she'd been listening and taking notes, so she carefully slipped the notebook and pen back into her pocket and began to move away. But then she heard Rumpelstiltskin say, 'And I heard something weird the night Rosalind fell.'

'What did you hear?' whispered one of the dancing gingerbread men.

'I came back to the theatre after everyone had gone because I'd left my hotel key in the dressing room when Mrs Bagnell had been doing my make-up. When I was in there looking for it I heard laughing. It was weird *ghostly* laughing. It sounded like it was coming from the dressing room next door so I went to see who was in there. It was empty but the whole time I was in the room it felt like there was someone watching me.'

[15]

A Midnight Meeting

'Something just touched me!' screamed Pam, jumping up.

'Ouch! MY FOOT!' yelled Barbara.

'Shhhhhhhhhhh!' hissed Peter. 'You're going to get us all caught!'

The Secret Seven were allowed to use the shed at the bottom of Peter and Janet's garden to have their secret meetings. But they definitely weren't allowed to be there at midnight.

'Nothing touched you,' said Peter. 'You're just imagining it because Janet told us a made-up story about a laughing ghost! Let's get started. Jack's obviously not coming. His mum must've spotted him trying to sneak out.'

'Hey!' said Janet, crossly. 'I didn't make anything up. I told you all exactly what I heard, Peter!'

'No, I didn't mean you, Janet,' said Peter.

'I meant that Rumpelstiltskin made the laughing ghost up.'

'Just because you don't believe in ghosts, Peter, doesn't mean everyone who tells a ghost story is making it up,' said Pam.

George nodded.

'So you three still think there's a theatre ghost?' said Peter. 'You don't think it's Finola and this Rumpelstiltskin out to sabotage the play?'

George shrugged. 'I think it might be both,' he said. 'It's getting a bit weird at the theatre. I overheard someone say they saw a strange green light on the wall in their dressing room just before the show tonight!'

Pam gasped.

Peter closed his eyes and took a deep breath. 'I think some of these actors are letting their imaginations get the better of them since this ghost rumour has been going around,' he said. 'It was probably just light from a lamp or something.'

'Janet,' said Pam, gripping Janet's hand tightly. 'Have you heard any ghostly laughing when you've been down there with Mrs Bagnell?'

'No,' said Janet. 'Peter's right. I think Rumpelstiltskin probably made that story up so that everyone thinks a ghost is responsible for everything that's happened and no one suspects Finola. He's maybe her boyfriend or something.'

Barbara nodded loads. 'He's always running around and bringing Finola coffee and calling her *dah-ling*.'

Barbara jumped up, pulling Pam with her, and the two of them began prancing around the shed saying, 'Finola, *daaaaah-ling*! You're such a wonderful shampoo model, *daaaaaaah-ling*! Let me kiss your hairy feet, *daaaaaaa-ling*!'

Peter shook his head. 'Can you please be serious for a minute? And did the two of you *really* need to wear your pyjamas to the meeting?'

Barbara and Pam stopped dancing.

'Peter!' said Barbara. 'It's a *midnight* meeting. What did you expect?'

Janet laughed and took out the notebook.

'OK,' she said. 'Does anyone actually know Mr *Daaaaaaah-ling's* real name?'

'Oh! Let me check the sandwich list,' said Colin. 'I tried to write down everyone's character names next to their names.' He took out the sandwich order list. 'Here he is. Smoked duck salad. His name's Harrow. He's not written his first name.'

'Well, I think we need to keep a close eye on *Mr Harrow*,' said Peter. 'How is the handwriting analysis going?' he asked Colin. 'How long do you think it'll take you to finish?'

'I'm actually almost done!' said Colin, excitedly. 'I did most of it while I was waiting for my mum and dad to fall asleep so I could sneak out.' He opened his backpack and took out a book.

Peter looked at the cover and laughed. 'Trust you to have a book on analysing handwriting!'

'I've got two actually. But this one's the best,' Colin said. 'There are only a few samples left to analyse so it won't take long. I'll finish it now.'

'Great,' said Peter. 'Now we need to decide

what we're going to do once we find out who wrote that note.'

'I think we should ask them,' said Barbara. 'Just go up to them when no one else is around and say that we know they wrote the note and ask them what it means. I'll do it.'

'That's probably the only thing we can do,' said Janet.

'Just be careful,' said Colin, looking up from his magnifying glass. 'Don't frighten them off. Witnesses sometimes get a bit nervous. And if it was a witness who wrote that note to Finola, they're obviously scared to come forward.'

'Colin's right,' said Peter. 'Maybe Janet or I should do it.'

'Hey!' said Barbara. 'What are you trying to say? I think I know how to talk to a witness. I've been part of the Secret Seven for just as long as you have!'

'Fine,' said Peter. 'Just don't mess it up, OK?'

Barbara rolled her eyes. 'ANYWAY!' she said, loudly. 'Did anyone else notice how nervous Finola seemed onstage tonight?'

'Yes!' said Pam. 'It looked like she almost forgot her lines at one point. And when we were backstage between scenes she kept staring at everyone. It was weird.'

'She was staring at everyone really strangely during lunch too,' said Janet. 'I think she's getting worried about the note and who might know her *secret.*'

Suddenly Colin started waving his arms around. 'A MATCH! I found a MATCH!' he cried.

'Are you sure?' asked Peter.

'I'm one hundred per cent sure!'

'Thank goodness! I mean, all that effort we put into making those sandwiches. I'd be gutted if we had nothing to show for it!'

Janet had to stop herself from laughing. Peter had literally made *one* sandwich!

Colin held up the note they'd found in Finola's dressing room. 'Here,' he said. 'Look at the "y" in "your". It's got a long, flicky tail.' Then he held up the lunch order list. 'Now look at the tuna sandwich order with "no mayo" underlined three times.'

Tuna sandwich — no mayo

Pam gasped. 'The "y" in "mayo" has the exact same curly tail bit!' she said.

'Exactly,' said Colin, smiling. 'It's a perfect match!'

'So who had the tuna sandwich without mayo?' asked Peter.

Colin stopped smiling. 'That's the problem. We've got four sandwiches without names next to them. And the tuna without mayo is one of them.'

'So what do we do now?' asked Jack.

Peter sighed. 'I guess I'll just have to ask Mum to make more sandwiches.'

'No! That's a terrible idea. We're not putting her through that again,' Janet said, firmly.

All of a sudden they heard barking.

'It's Scamper,' said Janet. 'He's in the kitchen. He must have heard a noise.'

Peter peeked out of the shed to see if there were any lights on in the farmhouse. 'No lights,' he said. 'But we should get inside quick in case Mum and Dad wake up and realise we're not there.'

Everyone grabbed their stuff and rushed out of the shed. But then, just as they were getting on their bikes, Peter spotted something and shone his torch into the field.

And that's when they all saw a hooded figure running away.

[16]

The Wig

'I think someone followed me and Barbara last night to the shed,' said Pam.

Peter whipped his head round to face Pam. 'Why didn't you say something when you got there?' he hissed.

'I didn't realise until now,' she said, wrapping her arms round herself. 'Does anyone else feel that draught?' she asked.

George nodded.

'It's the ghost,' said Pam.

Peter sighed. 'No, it's just a draught, Pam, because we're sitting in a mop cupboard in an old theatre full of draughts and cobwebs and rats!' Peter knew the minute he said 'rats' that he shouldn't have.

'RATS?' screamed Pam and Barbara at the same time.

'Shhhhhhhhhhhh!' whispered George. 'We're not supposed to be in here!'

'Anyway, back to what you were saying about being followed, Pam!' said Janet.

'I thought I heard a noise behind us when we were crossing the field. But I assumed it was Jack and that he was late and trying to catch up with us. I looked back but couldn't see him, so I just kept going. And then I forgot all about it.'

'Where *is* Jack?' asked Peter. 'He should be here by now. Especially since he wasn't at the meeting last night.'

'What if it was Finola?' asked George. 'What if she's on to us?'

'I think it's more likely it was Susie,' said Peter. 'It wouldn't be the first time she's spied on us in the shed!'

'But how would she have known about the midnight meeting?' asked Janet. 'She usually follows Jack to the meetings. But he wasn't there.'

Peter didn't get a chance to answer because just then the door flew open.

'There you all are,' said Finola, narrowing her eyes. 'What are you up to in here?'

'We were just rehearsing,' said Barbara, confidently.

'Yes!' said Pam. 'This is how we get into character. Barbara tells us ghost stories before we go onstage so that we all look scared.'

Finola crossed her arms. 'Oh, really? On you go then,' she said, looking at Barbara. 'Don't let me stop you from finishing your *ghost story*.'

Everyone looked at Barbara. Pam had really put her on the spot.

Barbara froze for a second but then she said, 'Um. So . . . the next day all the villagers searched the field, but they could find no trace of the blonde woman who'd been spotted running across it at midnight.'

Pam's mouth dropped wide open.

Peter stared at Janet and she stared right back at him.

'And everyone knew that she'd never be seen again,' said Barbara, creepily. 'Because the theatre ghost had *got her*! The end.'

The Seven sat in silence, stunned.

Finola glared down at Barbara, her mouth set in a firm line.

Barbara glared right back at her.

'You're all needed onstage. Now!' Finola said. And then she flicked her long hair and stormed off.

Pam's mouth was still wide open.

'What was *that*?' hissed Peter.

Barbara stood up and brushed the dust off her trousers. 'If it *was* her spying on us last night, I want her to know we're not scared of her,' she said.

'But we are scared of her,' said George. 'Really, *really* scared!'

'Well, I'm not,' said Barbara. 'She's a bully. And it's time we stopped her.'

'Do you think it was Finola we saw running away last night?' asked Colin as they watched the play from the wings later.

'Maybe,' said Peter. 'I didn't think so at first, but she seemed quite annoyed by Barbara's story, didn't she?'

Colin nodded.

'Why does she keep doing that?' asked Peter. He was looking at Finola. Nothing had gone wrong with the play so far, but Finola was acting strangely. She kept touching her head and fiddling with her hair.

'She's probably worried she's close to getting caught,' said Colin. 'It looks like nervous behaviour.'

Colin and Peter watched as Finola began scratching her head. Then suddenly she stopped mid-sentence, dropped her *Little Red Riding Hood* basket and began clawing at her head with both hands.

'Something's wrong,' said Peter.

They watched as Finola started screaming and continued to claw at her head until her long hair came clean off and went flying into the stalls.

'MY WIG!' screamed Finola.

The audience gasped as the wig hit someone in the third row.

Everyone watched as Finola staggered around the stage, furiously scratching at her short black hair.

'Finola! Be careful!' someone cried.

But it was too late. Finola tripped over the

wolf's tail and fell backwards into the gingerbread house, which collapsed around her with a loud crunch.

The audience sat in shock as Finola clawed her way out.

'It was YOU!' she screamed, staggering to her feet and pointing off into the wings. 'YOU SABOTAGED MY PERFORMANCE! YOU PUT ITCHING POWER IN MY WIG, DIDN'T YOU?'

Pam and Barbara looked to see who Finola was pointing at. It was Mrs Bagnell, who was watching the play from the wings!

'What?' hissed Mrs Bagnell. 'I did no such thing! I had no idea you even *wore* a wig! You're a big shampoo model, after all!'

The audience began to whisper loudly about Finola and her wig. They'd all seen her poster up in town.

'Yes you did! You were staring at my hair when you were doing my make-up. I saw you!' shrieked Finola. '*You* were the one who sent me that note about knowing my secret, weren't you? You've ALWAYS hated me, haven't you?'

The audience watched the events unfold onstage in shocked silence. Barbara wondered if they thought this was part of the play. But then the director shouted, 'GET THAT CURTAIN DOWN NOW!'

[17]

A Delicious Picnic

'I can't believe I missed all the action!' said Jack the next day, stuffing his face with his third cheese and jam sandwich. He had missed out on last night's performance, so the others were filling him in. 'Does she really wear a wig?'

Barbara nodded. 'Everyone was pretty shocked,' she said. 'I mean, she goes on and on about her hair and how she's a shampoo model. *All the time.*'

'I overheard someone say that she might lose her job as a shampoo model if more people find out,' said Pam.

'What happened after she accused Mrs Bagnell?' asked Jack.

'She stormed straight out of the theatre,' said Pam. 'She didn't even change out of her costume!'

'Do you think it was Mrs Bagnell who messed with her wig?' asked Jack.

'Absolutely not!' said Janet. 'She wouldn't do that. Plus, I helped Mrs Bagnell do Finola's make-up and I never noticed she was wearing a wig, so I don't think Mrs Bagnell would have either.'

'But why was she so sure it was Mrs B then?' asked Jack.

'Because she knows Mrs Bagnell doesn't like her very much after what happened with Adaline,' said Janet.

'So does this mean we got it all wrong?' asked Jack. 'Finola isn't anything to do with it?'

'She must have been telling the *truth* about getting locked in her dressing room during Rosalind's accident!' said Janet.

Colin nodded. 'I think so. It looks like the note was about Finola's wig. I think whoever's sabotaging the play must be the one who sent Finola the note and put the itching powder in her wig.'

Jack's eyes went wide. 'But who?'

'That's what we need to figure out,' said Peter.

'But first we eat!' said Janet, taking a final box of food out of the picnic basket.

'This picnic is amazing!' said Pam.

Pam was right. Peter and Janet's mum had said they were spending too much time indoors and had decided to make them an extra-special picnic. She'd wrapped it all up in her fanciest picnic basket and had told them to go outside and enjoy the fresh air.

There were ham sandwiches, cheese and jam sandwiches, freshly baked mini sausage rolls, apple and blackberry tarts, cheese and pickled onions on sticks, a raspberry and white chocolate sponge cake, homemade lemonade and chunks of Scottish tablet wrapped in a cloth napkin.

'And I brought some chocolate coconut truffles my dad made,' said Barbara.

Jack gasped when he saw them. They looked like something from a fancy chocolate shop!

The Secret Seven tucked into the delicious picnic.

'I think these might be the best sandwiches I've ever eaten,' said Jack, stuffing another cheese and jam sandwich into his mouth.

'They're good,' said Peter. 'But they're not *that* good. It's because you haven't eaten anything in twenty-four hours.'

'Worst twenty-four hours of my life,' said Jack, lying out flat on the grass while he licked jam off his fingers.

'Mum made a giant macaroni cheese pie. She used *five* different types of cheese and topped it off with this amazing onion jam thing she makes. And I couldn't have *any* of it. I was gutted. She only does it twice a month. I'll have to wait *another two whole weeks* for a slice!'

'I take it you're feeling back to your old self then?' said Janet as Jack popped another sandwich into his mouth.

Jack nodded. 'I'm fine now but my tummy felt awful. Susie thinks it could have been food poisoning. Same as the special-effects guys I guess,' he said, helping himself to a handful of sausage rolls.

Just then Scamper barked loudly. He was staring at the picnic basket.

Janet laughed. 'I'm sure there's a little something in here for you too,' she said.

Scamper watched closely as she reached into the basket and brought out a tub that said 'Scamper' on it. He started to whimper with excitement.

'Here you go, boy,' said Janet. 'Mum's given you the extra-tasty doggy biscuits today!'

Scamper munched greedily on a fancy dog biscuit and then put his paw up to ask for another one a few seconds later.

'What's that smell?' asked Pam.

'It wasn't me,' said Jack, still munching away.

Peter leant over and gave Scamper a sniff. 'It's Scamper. He's a bit smelly,' he said. 'We should give him a bath.'

Scamper got up off the picnic rug and walked towards a big tree.

Jack laughed out loud. 'Ha! He's in a huff because Peter called him smelly!'

'No,' said Janet. 'It's because Peter said B. A. T. H.'

Just then Scamper started growling.

'It's OK, Scamper!' Peter called after him. 'Come back, boy.'

But Scamper didn't move.

George gulped. 'I think there's someone behind the tree,' he whispered.

[18]

Who's Gate-Crashing the Picnic?

Scamper was staring at the big tree.

Jack jumped up and put his finger to his lips to let everyone else know he wanted them to be quiet.

The rest of the Seven watched in silence as he tiptoed towards Scamper.

'Come out!' Jack yelled when he reached the tree. 'We know you're there. Scamper can smell your stinking feet from here!'

Binkie stuck her head out from behind the tree. 'MY FEET DON'T STINK!' she shouted back.

'How long have you been there?' demanded Peter.

'We got here first!' said Binkie, crossing her arms. 'So maybe *you're* the ones spying on us! Did you ever think of that?'

'That doesn't even make any sense, Binkie,' said Janet.

'What do you mean "we"?' said Jack as he peered behind the tree trunk. He was looking for his annoying little sister.

'Um, I meant *me.* Not *we,*' said Binkie, nervously.

'Nice try,' said Peter. 'Where's Susie?'

'NOWHERE!' yelled Binkie, and then she turned and ran across the field towards the farmhouse.

Jack looked at Peter. 'Should we go after her?' he asked.

'No point. She obviously heard everything we said anyway. Right, back to the meeting,' Peter said, sitting back down on the picnic rug. 'I have another idea about who might be behind all the strange goings-on at the theatre. And I think it might be time to go to the police!'

'*What?*' said Colin. 'Why didn't you say something before now? Have you got evidence?'

Peter nodded. His eyes were wide. 'I have an eyewitness who says they saw this person steal the trapdoor key and they're willing to tell the police exactly what they saw.'

Everyone was in shock at what Peter had just said.

'*Who?*' said Jack.

'I don't want to upset you or anything, Jack. But it's Susie.'

Pam gasped.

'VERY FUNNY, PETER!' a voice yelled from above.

The Seven looked up at the tree just as Susie poked her head out from between the branches.

'SUSIE!' shouted Jack. 'GET DOWN HERE NOW!'

'I'm coming down,' she said. 'But not because *you've* asked me to.'

'How did you know she was up there?' asked Janet.

Peter shrugged. 'It was the only place she could be,' he said. 'There isn't anywhere else to hide out here.'

Susie landed with a thump, walked over to the picnic blanket and helped herself to a chocolate coconut truffle.

'Hey! Those aren't for you!' said Jack.

'Fine,' said Susie. 'They're disgusting anyway.'

Janet was furious. She didn't often feel this way but if there was one person who could really wind her up, it was Susie. She was just so *rude*.

'We saw you the other night, you know,' said Peter. 'At midnight? Crossing the field?'

Susie smiled. 'I'm sure I don't know what you're talking about, Peter,' she said.

'And Pam heard you following her!' said Peter, crossly. 'How did you know about the midnight meeting anyway?'

'There was a midnight meeting?' asked Jack. 'Why didn't I get an invite?'

'You did,' said Peter. 'We put a letter through your door, but we thought your mum and dad must have stopped you when you didn't come.'

Jack stared at Susie. 'I didn't get that,' he said. 'I wonder why?'

Peter was furious. 'SUSIE!' he yelled. 'That was an official Secret Seven letter! And it was clearly addressed to JACK, not YOU!'

'I think you should go, Susie,' said Janet, firmly.

'I will,' said Susie, taking a seat on the blanket. 'Soon.'

Jack looked like he was going to burst.

'But first, come and sit down, Jack,' Susie said, patting the blanket with her hand. 'I'm here on official Terrific Two business.'

'No way!' said Jack.

'You sure?' she said. 'I have some information that might be very useful to you. You know, since you've got it all wrong!'

'Fine,' said Jack. 'Tell us what you know.'

'I know quite a lot,' said Susie. 'In fact, I know so much that the Terrific Two might be making a trip to see the police inspector so they can arrest the culprit.'

'Really?' asked Janet. 'And who might the culprit be then?'

Susie turned to face Janet and smirked at her. 'Out of everyone you really should have figured this out by now,' said Susie.

'Why me?' asked Janet.

But Susie just smiled.

'Look, Susie,' said Janet, 'are you actually

going to tell us anything or are you just going to sit there being annoying?'

'Oh, *well*,' said Susie, huffily. 'If you're going to be like *that*, Janet, then I'll go.'

'Wait,' said Colin. 'Who do you think the culprit is?'

'She doesn't have a clue who it is!' said Peter. 'If she did, she wouldn't be spying on our meeting!'

'I *do* know who it is,' said Susie. 'It's Mrs Bagnell!'

'What!' said Janet. 'You're wrong!'

'No,' said Susie. 'I'm not wrong actually. And I can prove it.'

'Go on then,' said Peter.

'Fine,' said Susie. 'Have any of you even bothered to notice that every time something goes wrong Mrs Bagnell is there watching?' Susie looked at Janet. 'Even though she's supposed to be downstairs in the dressing room with *you* sorting out the make-up and stuff for the scene changes?'

Janet was furious. Susie didn't know what she was talking about! 'She sometimes nips up to watch because she wants to see the play,' said Janet. 'That's all!'

Susie smirked. 'Well, what about the fact that *she's* the one who started the whole ghost rumour? She's obviously trying to trick people into thinking it's a ghost so no one will suspect her! I heard her tell everyone that the theatre was haunted by a ghost and that she'd spotted it in her dressing room.'

'Mrs Bagnell did not say she's seen a ghost in the dressing room!' said Janet. 'You're making that up!'

'Am not!' said Susie. 'Ask anyone that was there! And there's more,' she added.

Janet looked at Colin. He was writing everything that Susie said down in the Secret Seven notebook. 'Don't bother writing this down,' said Janet. 'She's obviously making the whole thing up!'

Colin looked Peter.

Peter nodded at Colin to keep on writing and gave Janet a sheepish look.

'Wait a minute,' said Janet, 'you're not all believing this, are you?'

'Not yet,' said Peter. 'But go on, Susie.'

'And then there's the wig thing! Finola said it was definitely Mrs Bagnell who put itching powder in her wig. We interviewed her ourselves!' said Susie, proudly.

Now it was Peter's turn to be furious. 'You've got no right to be going around conducting interviews!' said Peter. 'This is a Secret Seven investigation!'

'Well, you're not doing a very good job,' said Susie.

'No,' said Janet. 'You're the one who's not doing a very good job! Why would Mrs Bagnell sabotage the play?'

Susie's smile disappeared. 'No idea,' she said. 'I'm sure she's got her reasons. But that's not important.'

Colin stopped taking notes and slapped the notebook shut. 'Excuse me, Susie,' he said, 'but having a motive for committing a crime is *very* important.'

Susie smiled. 'But it's not the *most* important thing, is it?' she asked, grinning.

Colin knew that Susie was right. Motive *wasn't* the most important thing; evidence was.

'It was Mrs Bagnell who put the itching

powder in Finola's wig,' said Susie. 'And we can prove it!'

'She's lying,' said Jack. 'She doesn't know a thing.'

'I am not lying,' said Susie, firmly. 'Binkie saw Mrs Bagnell buy itching powder in the joke shop in town with her *own eyes*. And as soon as we tell the police, they'll be able to check with the shop owner!'

Peter looked at Janet and then back at Susie. If this was true, then he knew that it was strong evidence that Mrs Bagnell was involved.

'Go home, Susie!' shouted Janet. 'Mrs Bagnell is our FRIEND. I won't sit here and let you speak RUBBISH about her!'

'Fine,' said Susie, getting up. 'I know when I'm not wanted. And that dog smells, anyway.'

Scamper barked loudly and Susie jumped.

Janet couldn't help herself. 'You'd better watch out,' said Janet. 'We've got him well trained.'

Susie scowled at them and then ran off across the field.

[19]

The Blackout

'I can't believe Finola's gone,' whispered Pam later as she and Barbara watched the play from the wings. 'I overheard the director say that she stormed out last night after what happened and that she hasn't been seen since!'

'I heard someone say that she'd been called back down to London to have a meeting with the shampoo company she models for and that she might get sacked,' said Barbara.

'It's amazing that Farah has been able to play both parts tonight!' said Pam. 'She's a better Little Red Riding Hood than Finola. I didn't think she was very good at all.'

Something caught Barbara's attention. 'Do you smell that?' she said. 'Is that smoke?'

'Oh, no,' said Pam. 'Look!'

The girls watched as the stage began to fill with smoke.

'The smoke machine,' said Barbara. 'It's going haywire!'

'What should we do?' asked Pam.

Suddenly the director appeared. 'Have either of you seen Daniela or Taj?' he hissed. 'We need to get the smoke machine under control now!'

Pam and Barbara shook their heads and the director ran off.

'I have to go out in a second,' said Barbara. 'It's my scene!'

Just then Daniela appeared. 'Have you seen Taj?' she said. 'I can't get the smoke machine to stop!'

Pam and Barbara shook their heads.

'You'd better go,' said Daniela, pointing to the stage and then she ran off.

Barbara looked warily at Pam.

'It's OK,' said Pam. 'I'm sure the machine will stop in a minute. And it's not as though it's real smoke. Don't worry.' Then she added, 'Break a leg! Wait. Should I not say that because of the trapdoor? I'm not sure. OK, well, good luck! Oh, no! Is that bad luck?'

Barbara laughed. She could always trust

Pam to make her laugh (even when Pam didn't actually mean to make her laugh).

Barbara did a tiny roar at Pam and Pam roared back. 'And don't worry,' said Barbara. 'I don't think this show could get any more bad luck, do you?'

As soon as Barbara stepped onstage, she wished she hadn't said that. The smoke was much worse than it had looked from the wings. She stepped towards Farah, ready to deliver her speech about how the witch shouldn't eat her poor, beloved Hansel and Gretel.

'Oh, what a misty eve it is tonight!' said Farah, making up a few lines to try to keep the audience happy. 'I hope no one sneaks up on me while I boil these delicious children.'

The audience laughed, and Barbara relaxed a little. But then all of a sudden the lights went out and the theatre was flooded with darkness.

There were gasps and a few seconds of silence while everyone waited, expecting the lights to come back on. But they didn't.

'Stay exactly where you are!' called the director. 'I don't want anyone falling off the stage.'

Barbara stood frozen to the spot.

'Barbara!' Pam yelled from the wings. 'Are you OK?'

'I'm fine!' Barbara yelled back. 'Stay where you are, Pam.'

Barbara remembered that George was backstage too. And George was terrified of the dark.

'George!' she shouted. 'If you can hear me, DON'T PANIC! Everything is going to be—'

But Barbara didn't get a chance to finish her sentence. Something cold brushed against the side of her arm and a second later there were loud screams from the stalls.

Suddenly the lights came back on. Barbara looked at her arm. She was covered in something white. And so was most of the front row!

[20]

The Ghost Strikes!

Everyone from backstage came rushing out and on to the stage.

'Oh my goodness!' cried Pam. 'IS THAT PART OF THE GHOST ON YOUR ARM?'

Barbara sniffed her arm. 'It's paint!' she yelled back.

Some people in the audience were still screaming. The director and some of the actors rushed down the steps and into the stalls to help. 'Sorry, everyone, but I'm afraid tonight's performance is cancelled,' shouted the director, ushering people towards the exit. 'Speak to the box office about a refund on your way out . . .'

'Are you sure you're OK?' asked Peter. 'Here, take this off,' he said, helping Barbara out of her cardigan.

'I'm fine,' she said. 'I just have no idea what's happening!'

'It looks like someone caused the blackout

and then rushed onstage and threw paint into the audience,' said Jack.

Barbara looked at George. He was staring at something. 'George, are you OK?' she asked.

'Um. Who's that?' asked George.

Everyone followed George's gaze off into the wings.

There was a dark, hooded figure watching them.

Pam gasped. 'It's the THEATRE GHOST!'

The hooded figure stepped back into the shadows and disappeared.

Jack and Peter rushed backstage but the figure had gone.

'Who was that?' asked Colin as he and the others caught up with them.

'There's no one here,' said Jack. 'They must have used a secret door or something.'

'It's gone!' Barbara cried.

'What's gone?' asked Janet, appearing from nowhere.

'The ghost!' said Barbara. 'It covered my arm in white paint and threw some into the stalls!'

'Is that what the screaming was about?

I heard the noise from downstairs,' said Janet.

'Where's Scamper?' asked Peter.

'I left him in the dressing room.'

'With Mrs Bagnell?' said Peter.

'No,' said Janet. 'She left me about ten minutes ago.'

'Where did she go?' asked Peter.

'She didn't say,' Janet said, hesitantly.

She knew what Peter was thinking. He thought Mrs Bagnell might have been to blame for all of this.

'Look!' said Colin, bending down to pick something up. 'It's a hooded coat! The culprit must have taken it off!'

Colin began inspecting the coat.

'It's quite big and loose, but it looks like a woman's coat,' he said.

'Check the pockets,' said Jack. 'There might be a clue there.'

'Nothing in the pockets,' said Colin. 'But there are white marks on the cuffs. It must be paint! And it's got a hood. This is definitely the coat the culprit was wearing. And it looks as though the culprit is a woman.'

'Can I take a look?' asked Janet.

'You recognise the coat, don't you?' asked Peter.

'No,' said Janet. 'I don't.' Colin handed Janet the coat and she inspected the cuffs carefully. 'But I recognise these marks. It's not paint. It's plaster. Mrs Bagnell used it to make fake noses for Rumpelstiltskin and the witch.' She looked up at Peter.

'Look,' said Peter, 'I didn't want to say anything earlier, but you said yourself that Mrs Bagnell wasn't in the dressing room for quite a long time on the opening night.'

Janet went quiet. Mrs Bagnell had disappeared a number of times for much longer than she had said she would. Janet had assumed she was helping the actors or solving problems or watching the show. But now she wasn't so sure.

'And she actually does have a motive,' said Colin. 'You said yourself she really doesn't like Finola, or the company, because of what happened with that girl, Adaline.'

'She also knows about the secret corridor and secret door,' said Jack. 'There might be more. That could be how she escaped so quickly just now.'

Barbara nodded. 'And she might have used another secret passageway to get under the stage and open the trapdoor without being noticed.'

Janet listened. She knew what everyone was saying made sense, but something about it just didn't feel right.

'Why would Mrs Bagnell offer to help the company out if she doesn't even like them?' asked Peter, gently.

'To be nice!' said Janet. 'Because she's nice!'

Nobody said anything back. They just looked down at the floor.

'I'm sorry, Janet,' said Barbara. 'I really like Mrs Bagnell too. But I think Peter's right. It doesn't make sense that she would offer to help after what the company did to Adaline. You said yourself that she told you a lot of the people she used to work with are still part of the cast and that she doesn't like them much. So why take a job where she has to spend so much time with them?'

'No,' said Janet. 'Something about all this

feels off. Just because you don't like people doesn't mean you go around opening trapdoors and pushing trees on them!'

'She also poisoned my brother,' said Susie, stepping out from her hiding place behind the curtain with Binkie.

Jack's eyes went wide. 'What do you mean she *poisoned me*?'

'It was Mrs Bagnell who made the scones that gave everyone food poisoning,' she said.

'What makes you so sure it was the scones?' asked Peter.

'The scones were the only food that both the special-effects guys and Jack could have eaten. There was nothing else to eat here on the first day,' said Susie. 'We think she gave one to the make-up artist too so that she'd get sick. Then Mrs Bagnell could offer to step in to help so she could get on with the sabotage!'

Peter was shocked. He'd never admit it to Susie, but she'd done great detective work.

Peter looked at Janet. 'I'm sorry, Janet,' he said.

Janet nodded. She knew what they had to do. 'Fine,' she said. 'Let's go.'

Susie, Binkie and the Seven made their way down to the dressing room in silence but were met with a shock when they opened the door.

'Oh my goodness!' cried Janet. 'What happened in here?'

The Seven stared at the dressing room. It had been completely trashed. Everything on the dressing table was lying smashed on the floor and Mrs Bagnell's make-up case had been shattered into a million pieces.

Janet gasped. 'Oh, no! He's gone! Scamper's gone!'

[21]

Someone's Locked in the Cupboard!

'I left him in here with Mrs Bagnell!' Janet said, frantically. She could feel her heart beating hard in her chest.

'Mrs Bagnell must've trashed the place before she ran off,' said Susie. 'Her final act of revenge! She must've taken Scamper with her.'

'This doesn't make any sense!' said Janet. 'She wouldn't wreck her own make-up like this! And why would she steal Scamper?'

Just then the Seven heard barking and Scamper appeared at the door.

'THERE YOU ARE, BOY!' cried Janet.

Peter and Janet rushed to give Scamper a hug.

'Is he OK?' asked Janet.

Peter checked him over. 'He looks fine,' said Peter. 'I think whoever did this must've scared him off. Good boy for coming back, Scamper.'

Suddenly Colin spotted something on the floor and bent down to pick it up. It was a notepad with a shopping list written on it.

'Um. I think it might be time to go get the police inspector,' Colin said. 'Look!' He held the shopping list up and pointed to one of the items on it.

George gasped. 'It's the same handwriting!'

Colin nodded. 'The "y" in "yoghurt" has the same curly "y" as the threatening note Finola got and the tuna with no mayo sandwich order,' he said. 'It was Mrs Bagnell who sent the threatening note to Finola.'

Peter looked at Janet, who nodded. 'George,' he said, 'take Scamper and go and get the police inspector. We'll stay here.'

George held Scamper by the collar and rushed out.

'Did anyone else hear that?' asked Barbara.

Peter sighed. 'This isn't a good time for ghost nonsense, Barbara!'

'Shhhhhhhhh!' said Barbara. 'Just be quiet and listen!'

Peter listened. There was a muffled sound coming from somewhere.

'What is it?' asked Pam, nervously.

The muffled moaning sound got louder. It was coming from inside the room.

'Oh, no,' said Pam, grabbing Barbara by the arm. 'It's the laughing ghost in the wall! Mr Harrow was right!'

Janet walked around the room to see where the noise was coming from. It was the store cupboard! Janet turned the handle, but the door was locked. 'Hello?' she said. 'Is someone in there?'

A voice mumbled something back, but Janet couldn't make it out. 'Someone's trapped in here,' she said.

'Or *something's* trapped in there!' said Pam.

'I'll go and get help!' said Jack, rushing out.

'What if it *is* a ghost?' said Barbara. 'Should we really just let it out? Maybe Mrs Bagnell caught it trashing her dressing room, trapped it in there on purpose and went to get help!'

'Barbara's right! We need to get out of here!' Pam said.

Just then Jack came rushing back into the

room, followed by Daniela and some of the actors.

'Is someone really locked in there? Is it the ghost?' asked Farah.

'This theatre ghost is a menace!' said Mr Harrow.

Everyone watched as Daniela fiddled with her huge set of keys before eventually finding the right one and unlocking the door.

And that's when everyone gasped.

[22]

Inside the Cupboard

Janet and Daniela rushed into the cupboard.

'Oh my goodness!' said Janet. 'What happened? Are you OK?'

'I. Um. I don't know,' Mrs Bagnell replied, raising her hand to her forehead.

'Careful,' said Daniela. 'You've got a nasty cut on your head.'

'Someone was here,' said Mrs Bagnell. 'Help me up.'

'Maybe you should stay sitting down for now,' said Janet. 'Pam, can you get Mrs Bagnell a glass of water, please?'

Pam rushed out to get the water.

'Did you say someone was here?' Peter asked.

'Yes,' said Mrs Bagnell. 'I don't know. I mean, I don't know who it was. I didn't see them.'

'Just take your time,' said Janet. 'There's no rush.'

Mrs Bagnell touched her forehead again. 'Tissues,' she said. 'I went into the cupboard to get tissues. I heard someone coming up behind me. And then . . . and then . . . they pushed me! I must've hit my head,' she added, looking a little bewildered.

Peter rushed forward with a chair and helped Janet and Daniela to lift Mrs Bagnell up.

'Thank you,' she said, leaning back and taking a deep breath.

'I'll go and get the first-aid kit for your head,' said Daniela. 'I'll be back in a few minutes.'

'Thank you, dear,' said Mrs Bagnell. Then she looked around at the dressing room. 'My MAKE-UP!' she cried. 'It's RUINED! What on earth is going on?'

'I'm afraid we need to ask you some questions about that, Mrs Bagnell,' said Peter.

'PETER!' said Janet. 'Not now!'

'No, it's fine,' said Mrs Bagnell.

'Do you have any idea who pushed you?' asked Peter.

Janet was relieved. She'd been worried Peter was going tell Mrs Bagnell that they had suspected she was the culprit before they'd found her locked in the cupboard.

'I've no idea who it was,' said Mrs Bagnell. 'I didn't have time to turn round.'

'Is there anything you remember?' asked Colin. 'Anything at all?'

'Actually, yes. I do remember something,' she said. 'I remember hearing clicking as whoever it was walked towards me. They were moving quickly, and it sounded like they were wearing heels.'

Colin opened the notebook and wrote down:

Culprit is a woman. Evidence: women's coat AND heeled shoes.

But then Susie and Binkie pushed past Colin and stood in front of Mrs Bagnell with their arms folded.

'We're the Terrific Two,' said Susie, 'and we

think that you might have locked *yourself* in that cupboard!'

'SUSIE!' yelled Janet.

'We also think you're the one who's been sabotaging this play,' continued Susie, ignoring her. 'We think it was you who opened the trapdoor and tampered with the scenery and made everything go wrong onstage. And then you made up a story about the theatre being haunted and blamed everything on the ghost, didn't you?'

Mrs Bagnell looked shocked. 'I beg your pardon. I did no such thing!' she said. 'Why on earth would you think I was responsible?'

Susie took out her notepad. 'Well, first of all,' she said, flicking through the pages, 'you always seem to be suspiciously close to the action whenever anything goes wrong, instead of being down here in the dressing room.'

'I like to go up and watch the play whenever I can,' said Mrs Bagnell. 'That's not a crime, is it?'

'There's more,' said Susie.

'Is there?' said Mrs Bagnell.

'Yes,' said Susie. 'What about the food poisoning?'

'What about it?' said Mrs Bagnell.

'It was you, wasn't it? You did something to the scones so you could get rid of the make-up artist and take her place. And the special-effects guys, so there would be fewer people to see you tampering with the scenery and sabotaging the play,' said Susie. 'And you made my brother really sick, you know!'

Mrs Bagnell shook her head. 'I did bring scones on the first day, but they didn't make anyone sick! They weren't even homemade! I bought them from the bakery,' she added. 'And it can't have been the scones that gave the special-effects guys food poisoning, otherwise everyone who ate them would have got sick, wouldn't they? Myself included. And I'm pretty sure I saw you eat one too, young lady!

'And as for the make-up artist,' continued Mrs Bagnell, 'I found out this morning that she's pregnant. That's why she'd been feeling ill. It had nothing to do with scones.'

Mrs Bagnell turned to look at Jack. 'I think every time I've seen you recently you've had a scone in your mouth,' said Mrs Bagnell. 'Would that be right?'

Jack shrugged.

'How many did you actually eat?' asked Janet.

'Not sure, I lost count. Eight? Maybe nine?' said Jack.

'Well, there you go,' said Mrs Bagnell. 'That solves the mystery of Jack's upset stomach!'

Susie narrowed her eyes at Mrs Bagnell and tapped her notepad with her pen.

'Any more questions for me?' asked Mrs Bagnell, raising an eyebrow sarcastically.

'Yes, actually,' said Susie. 'You're the one who told everyone there was a theatre ghost sabotaging the play, aren't you? So people wouldn't suspect you.'

Mrs Bagnell looked down for a second. 'OK,' she said. 'You've got me.'

[23]

'A'

'I knew it!' said Susie.

Janet's heart leapt in her chest.

'I *did* spread the rumour about the ghost,' said Mrs Bagnell. 'But I only did it for fun. Some of those actors are incredibly annoying. I thought it would be amusing to let them think the place was haunted and watch them scare themselves silly. Now, have I managed to successfully clear my name yet?'

'Yes,' said Janet. 'That's enough, Susie!'

Susie looked at Mrs Bagnell square in the eye. 'Not quite,' she said. 'I have one more thing to say.'

Mrs Bagnell rolled her eyes.

'We have a witness,' said Susie, smugly.

'What *witness*?' asked Mrs Bagnell.

'I think I'll wait until the police get here to reveal that,' she said, shutting her notebook and stepping to the side.

'You called the police?' asked Mrs Bagnell.

Susie nodded. 'They're on their way.'

'Good!' said Mrs Bagnell. 'I'm pleased to hear that. Then maybe we can stop this nonsense and find out who attacked me!'

Peter looked at Janet. He wanted Mrs Bagnell to be innocent just as much as she did. But he knew there were still a few things that hadn't been explained.

'Mrs Bagnell,' said Peter, gently, 'before the police get here, there are just a couple of things we still don't understand.'

Mrs Bagnell turned to face Janet.

'Am I under investigation by the Secret Seven too?' she asked.

Janet shook her head. 'No. Definitely not,' she said, firmly. 'I think Peter just wants to ask you about the itching powder and the note you gave Finola.'

Mrs Bagnell looked puzzled.

'Binkie says she saw you buying itching powder from the joke shop in town on the same day someone sabotaged Finola's wig,' said Peter.

'No she did NOT!' said Mrs Bagnell. 'I did

visit the joke shop that day, but I was picking up a new fake moustache for Rumpelstiltskin's costume.' She pointed at Mr Harrow who was standing in the corner of the room listening intently. 'I certainly didn't buy itching powder. You can ask the shop owner yourself if you don't believe me!'

'We believe you,' said Janet.

Peter turned to face Binkie. 'You said you saw Mrs Bagnell buy the itching powder with your own eyes,' he said.

'Well, I did, yes. Sort of,' said Binkie, looking a little unsure. 'I saw her go in and buy *something*. I'm sure it must have been itching powder. It's the only place you can buy it in town!'

'Susie!' said Jack. 'Did you know about this?'

Susie shrugged.

Peter shook his head. 'And that's why neither of you could ever be members of the Secret Seven!' said Peter. 'If you ask me, you should be called the *Terrible* Two!'

'Come on, Binkie,' said Susie. 'We've got another mystery we need to solve anyway. Let's get out of here.'

'Yeah!' said Binkie.

And they both ran out.

'Well,' said Mrs Bagnell. 'That was unpleasant!'

'I'm so sorry, Mrs Bagnell,' said Janet. She felt awful. She had no idea who had been sabotaging the play, but she was one hundred per cent sure it wasn't Mrs Bagnell.

'Where is that stagehand with the first-aid kit?' yelled Mr Harrow. 'Mrs Bagnell's bleeding half to death here.'

'I'm fine,' said Mrs Bagnell, picking up a cotton wool ball and dabbing her head with it. 'It's just a scratch. And, *please*, would you stop calling her "that stagehand". Her name is Daniela.'

Mr Harrow frowned and folded his arms.

'Mrs Bagnell,' said Colin, holding up the notepad he found on the floor, 'is this your shopping list?'

'Yes,' said Mrs Bagnell. 'Why do you ask?'

'Um,' said Colin, 'it's just we've seen this handwriting somewhere else.'

'Well, you'll have to ask Daniela about that

when she gets back,' said Mrs Bagnell. 'That's her handwriting, not mine.'

The Seven looked at each other.

'Wait,' said Janet, taking the notepad from Colin. 'Daniela wrote this? You're sure?'

'Yes, I'm sure,' said Mrs Bagnell. 'She wrote it for me earlier today when I couldn't find my glasses. What does this have to do with anything?'

'We found a threatening note in Finola's dressing room,' said Janet. 'It's the same handwriting.'

'You had no right snooping around in Finola's dressing room! No wonder she left!' said Mr Harrow, angrily.

'Wait just a second,' said Mrs Bagnell, getting up from her chair. 'You think Daniela had something to do with Finola's wig?'

Janet nodded. 'I do,' she said. 'In fact, if that's her handwriting, I think she's the one who's been sabotaging this play since the opening night.'

'No. It can't be her,' said Mrs Bagnell. 'Daniela is a lovely girl! She brings me a coffee and cake every afternoon and she won't take a penny for it. She wouldn't sabotage the play. And she can't have been the one who did this to me!'

'Of course it was her,' said Mr Harrow. 'She's the only one with a key for that cupboard you were locked in!'

'I'm so sorry, Mrs Bagnell,' said Janet.

Mrs Bagnell sat back down.

'It makes sense,' said Peter. 'Daniela knows how to operate the trapdoor and she had access to the scenery and all the props.'

'But why would she want to sabotage the play?' asked Mrs Bagnell.

Janet looked down at the pad in her hands. She hadn't noticed it before but there was a tiny 'A' monogramed at the bottom of the page.

'Is this one of your notepads?' she asked Mrs Bagnell.

'No, it's Daniela's,' said Mrs Bagnell. 'She left it here earlier today. I meant to take the page out and give it back to her.'

Janet stared at the 'A'. Why would Daniela have a notepad decorated with the letter 'A'?

Janet flicked through the notepad. It was empty.

But then she noticed something. The front page was indented as though someone had been pressing really hard when they had written on the page before it.

'I need a pencil,' said Janet. 'Quickly!'

George grabbed a make-up pencil from the floor and handed it to Janet.

Janet began shading in the page lightly with the pencil until writing appeared. She stared at the page. It was Daniela's name, written over and over again in different ways. Sometimes the 'D' was large, other times it was small.

Pam peeked over Janet's shoulder. 'Was she practising her signature maybe?' she asked.

Janet shook her head. 'No,' she said. 'She'd have written her surname too if she was doing that.'

Janet stared at Daniela's name. It was almost like she was practising how to write her first name, which Janet found odd. She looked down at the 'A' and back at the name 'Daniela' and gasped. She'd just noticed something. 'No,' she said. 'It can't be!'

'What?' said Peter. 'What have you found?'

Janet flicked to the next blank page and started writing something down with the make-up pencil.

'You shouldn't be writing on that!' said Colin. 'That's tampering with evidence!'

Janet stared at what she had written. She couldn't believe it. She was right!

'There's an "A" embossed at the bottom of each page of the pad,' said Janet. 'I couldn't understand why. But then I noticed something about the name "Daniela" when I kept looking at it written in different ways.'

Janet held up what she had written for everyone to see.

And it said:

DANIELA
ADALINE

'Daniela is an anagram of Adaline,' said Janet. 'That can't just be a coincidence. Can it?'

'Wait,' said Jack. 'So you mean . . . What do you mean?'

'I think Daniela *is* Adaline!' she said.

'No, she can't be!' said Mrs Bagnell. 'I would have recognised her!'

'You said it's been about ten years since you worked with the theatre company,' said Janet. 'Adaline was only a child. She would have changed a lot since then. Colin, can I see the sandwich order list for a moment?'

Colin took the list out of his pocket and handed it to her.

Janet looked at the tuna sandwich (no mayo) order. '"No mayo" was underlined three times,' she said. 'Mrs Bagnell, the story you told me about Adaline, you said she had a nasty allergic reaction. It was eggs she was allergic to, wasn't it?'

'Yes,' said Mrs Bagnell. 'Why?'

'Daniela ordered a tuna sandwich,' said Janet. 'And she wrote "no mayo" next to it and underlined it three times. Maybe that was because she's allergic to eggs.'

'It's her!' said Barbara. 'It's Adaline! She came back to get revenge on Finola and everyone else for what they did to her!'

'Does Daniela remind you of Adaline at all?' Janet asked Mrs Bagnell.

'I don't know,' said Mrs Bagnell. 'It was a long time ago. She'd be nineteen or twenty years old by now. Which I suppose is the same age as Daniela.' She closed her eyes and rubbed her temples. 'This is all so strange. But now that I really think about it, there is something familiar about Daniela. Adaline had long red hair, but I suppose she could have easily cut it short and dyed it brown as she grew up, couldn't she?'

'She probably changed her hair so no one here would recognise her,' said Barbara.

'But why would she do all of this?' asked Mrs Bagnell. 'Surely not just because Finola stole her leading role as a child, would she?'

'It looks that way,' said Janet.

Mrs Bagnell shook her head again. 'I can't believe this is happening,' she said. 'Could Daniela really be Adaline?'

'Yes,' said Daniela, appearing in the doorway. 'It's me.'

[24]

A Blast from the Past

Everyone stared at Daniela.

'Adaline?' said Mrs Bagnell. 'Is that really you?'

'Yes,' said Adaline.

'It was you,' said Peter, stepping forward. 'You opened the trapdoor, didn't you? And then you hid the spare key and pretended that it had been stolen.'

Adaline stared at Peter.

'And you're the hooded figure who threw paint on me!' said Barbara.

'Yes,' she said. 'It was me. It was all me.'

And then she turned to face the group of actors watching her with wide eyes. 'I'm the one who sabotaged your stupid play! And you all deserved it!' she shouted. 'You ruined my CAREER. But I didn't do this to you, Mrs Bagnell. I would never.' And then she turned and ran.

'Stay here, we'll be back,' Peter said to the others. And then he and Jack ran out after her.

'This is outrageous!' yelled Mr Harrow. 'She can't be allowed to get away with this!'

Mr Harrow carried on ranting until the police inspector and an officer arrived with George and Scamper.

Scamper began growling as soon as George led him into the room.

'It's OK, boy,' said Janet, bending down to pet him. 'It's all over now.'

'Hallo,' said the police inspector. 'What's been going on here then?'

The children explained what had happened with the trapdoor and about Adaline.

'And you were attacked, Mrs Bagnell?' the police inspector asked.

'Yes,' said Mrs Bagnell. 'But not by Daniela, I mean, Adaline. Either way, it wasn't her. It was someone else.'

'Do you have any idea who it might have been who attacked you?' he asked.

'OF COURSE IT WAS ADALINE!' yelled Mr Harrow. 'She's a LIAR!'

Scamper growled loudly at Mr Harrow.

'And what is that *mutt* doing in here?' continued Mr Harrow. 'Are dogs even allowed in the theatre? GET IT OUT!'

The police inspector turned to face Mr Harrow. 'I'd ask you to stay calm, please, sir,' he said.

'CALM?' shouted Mr Harrow. 'We've just found out that someone has been sabotaging us! Why are you standing here? You should be out there trying to CATCH HER!'

Scamper moved forward and barked loudly at Mr Harrow.

Scamper really didn't like Mr Harrow. Peter was beginning to wonder if it was just because he was yelling so much or whether there was another reason.

'All in good time, sir,' said the police inspector.

'Well, I'm going to look for her if you won't,' said Mr Harrow, walking towards the door.

George gasped.

'What?' said Mr Harrow, turning round.

George was staring at Mr Harrow's feet. He

was wearing old-fashioned heeled shoes as part of his Rumpelstiltskin outfit.

'Your shoes,' said George. 'They sound like clicking heels.'

Mr Harrow looked up at Mrs Bagnell and then tried to run out, but the police inspector blocked the exit.

'I knew you were behaving suspiciously!' said the police inspector. 'What's going on?'

'I thought it was you!' said Mr Harrow, pointing at Mrs Bagnell. 'I thought *you* were the one who put itching powder in my darling Finola's wig. I was SURE of it! I wanted you to pay for what you did to her. She's lost her modelling contract because of it!'

'So you locked me in a cupboard and destroyed my make-up?'

Mr Harrow looked at the even larger group of actors that had now formed outside the dressing-room door.

'What's going on in here?' asked the director. 'What's all the shouting about?'

'And YOU!' yelled Mr Harrow. 'You *never* appreciated how talented my darling Finola is. Well, now you've got what you deserve. You all have! Finola has finally left the company. And you'll all be lost without her!'

'That's what you meant when we heard you through the wall,' said Pam. 'You said that everyone would soon be sorry they didn't appreciate Finola more. You meant because she was leaving.'

'You're absolutely right I did! She was the star of this show and this *amateur* of a director was planning to give Finola's part to Farah and we knew it!'

'OK,' said the police inspector, 'I think we've heard quite enough from you. You're taking a trip to the police station. Out you go.'

Everyone watched as Mr Harrow was put in handcuffs and taken away by the police officer.

'Now,' said the police inspector, 'Janet, do you have any idea where I might find this Adaline?'

Janet shook her head. 'I'm not sure. She ran out just before you got here. Peter and Jack went to look for her.'

'I see,' he said, taking his notepad out. 'Well, if you could give me a description, I'm sure she won't get far.'

Janet and the others gave him the best description they could.

Just then Peter and Jack came back. 'We couldn't find her anywhere,' they said. 'We checked everywhere we could think of. She's gone.'

'Don't worry,' said the police inspector. 'We'll find her. OK, everyone, out of the theatre, please. We need to do a full search.'

'Can I have a few minutes in here to sort this mess out?' asked Mrs Bagnell.

'Of course,' said the police inspector. 'The Secret Seven can stay and give you a hand.'

'Thank you,' said Janet, shaking his hand.

'No problem,' said the police inspector. 'Thank you all for your great work solving this crime. Sometimes I don't know what we'd do without you lot. Thank goodness for the Secret Seven!'

'Are you feeling OK?' Janet asked Mrs Bagnell after everyone except the Seven had left.

'No,' said Mrs Bagnell, her eyes filling with tears. 'I'm not. I'm upset about Adaline. I can't believe she's the one who did all this. She used to be such a sweet girl. It breaks my heart to think she's been so resentful all these years. I wish I'd had a chance to talk to her. And who knows where she is or what will happen to her now!'

Suddenly Barbara remembered something. 'I think I know where Adaline is,' she said. 'Follow me.'

[25]

The Secret Room

Everyone followed Barbara into the dressing room next door.

'Why are we in here?' asked Janet.

Barbara looked carefully around the room.

'Do you remember the story Janet overheard Mr Harrow telling everyone? About the laughing ghost?'

'Oh, no,' said George. 'I thought there wasn't a ghost any more! Are you saying that you think there's a ghost again?'

'Calm down,' said Barbara. 'I definitely *do* think there's a ghost.' Pam gasped. 'But that's not what I'm talking about just now.'

Everyone watched as Barbara walked around the room, inspecting the walls closely.

'Mr Harrow said that when he came in here to see where the laughing noise was coming from that the room was empty but he felt like he was being watched,' said Barbara. 'Do you remember that?'

Everyone nodded, especially George.

Barbara turned to face them. 'Well, I think he was right. I think he was being watched,' she said, quietly. 'But not by a ghost. I think he was being watched by Adaline. And I think she's watching us right now!'

Barbara pointed to the poster on the wall. 'Interesting eyes that actress has, aren't they?' she whispered.

Everyone looked at the poster. One of the actress's eyes looked hollow.

Barbara put her hand on the light switch. 'Don't scream, Pam. OK?'

'Um, OK,' said Pam, nervously.

Then Barbara hit the switch and the light went out.

'Look at the poster,' hissed Barbara.

Pam did a tiny gasp. 'There's a green light shining out of her eye!' she whispered.

'It's a peephole,' said Colin.

'There's something behind that wall!' said Jack. 'Wait. What is it? It can't be the secret corridor. That's on the opposite wall.'

Barbara switched the light back on and walked over to the poster. 'Only one way to find out,' she said. And then she pressed against the poster a few times until something clicked and the door swung open to reveal a small room.

'Adaline!' said Mrs Bagnell.

'Mrs Bagnell,' said Adaline, quietly.

'Can we talk to you?' asked Mrs Bagnell.

Adaline was sitting on the floor in the corner of the dimly lit room hugging her knees. 'I suppose so,' she said. 'You've found me now.'

Mrs Bagnell ducked through the doorway and sat down next to her. 'Are you all right?' she asked.

Adaline shook her head and began to cry. 'They ruined my life, Mrs Bagnell. And they didn't even care! I couldn't get another acting part after that. It took me months to get back enough confidence to actually go to another audition. And when I did I froze. I haven't managed to get an acting job since. What Finola and the company did to me ruined my acting career. And now, instead of being onstage, starring in a show, I'm a stagehand. They stole my dream. They deserved everything they got – epsecially Finola!' said Adaline, bitterly.

'But how did you know about Finola's wig?' asked Janet.

'I'd been in and out of her dressing room enough times to have worked it out. And I covered her wig with itching powder that night so that she'd lose her role, and everything would be taken away from her – just like it was from me!' Adaline let out a sob.

'Adaline,' said Mrs Bagnell, 'you're right. It isn't fair what they did to you. But this isn't OK. People were hurt. And poor Rosalind wasn't even part of the company when you worked with them.'

'I know. I never meant to hurt Rosalind,' said Adaline. 'Finola was supposed to be onstage. I had no idea that her understudy had stepped in to do her scene. I was already under the stage.'

'But you meant to hurt Farah, didn't you?' said Peter. 'That's why you wouldn't let me or Colin touch the scenery, isn't it? You didn't want us to find out that you'd tampered with the tree after Taj had checked it, did you?'

'And it was you I saw backstage, wasn't it?' said Jack. 'You were wearing a white sheet or something and pretending to be the theatre ghost!'

Daniela nodded. 'Everyone already thought the theatre was haunted because of the rumours. It was easy to make them think it was a ghost sabotaging their play. All I had to do was change the smoke machine settings and fiddle with the curtain pull and it looked like everything was happening by itself. I knew they'd all think it was a ghost.'

'And you gave the special-effects guys something that gave them food poisoning, didn't you?' asked Colin. 'So you could be in charge of operating everything?'

Adaline nodded and began to cry again.

'Adaline,' said Mrs Bagnell, firmly. 'You need to confess to the police and get your life back on track. There's no other way out of this.'

Adaline sniffled and hiccupped through her tears.

'Oh, Adaline,' said Mrs Bagnell. 'It's time to make a change. You can't live like this. And I can help you. Please let me help you, dear.'

Just then the police inspector walked into the dressing room.

'I'm sorry, Mrs Bagnell,' said Adaline. 'Thank you for trying to help me.' And then she opened another door in the secret room and closed it behind her before anyone could stop her.

The police inspector rushed over and tried to open the door Adaline had left through but it wouldn't move.

'She must have locked it from the other side,' said Peter.

'Stand back,' said the police inspector, and he pushed his shoulder against the door until it burst open.

Jack leant forward and peeked through the doorway. 'I can't believe this,' he said. 'It's another corridor. And it's empty. She's gone.'

[26]

The Return of the Theatre Ghost!

'Well, those actors must've enjoyed my sandwiches after all because news has spread!' said Peter and Janet's mum the next morning as she made a plate of sandwiches, jam tarts and ginger biscuits for the Secret Seven meeting. 'And guess what? I've been offered a job catering lunch for a party in the village hall next month. It's for over seventy people!'

'Are you going to take it?' asked Peter, helping himself to a ginger biscuit.

'I already have,' she said. 'And guess whose turn it is to ask for a favour?'

Peter groaned. He loved eating sandwiches, but he really hated making them.

'Maybe you should open your own sandwich and cake shop,' said Janet, excitedly.

'I'm not sure about that,' she said, laughing.

'I like being at home on the farm, in my own kitchen.'

'You could start your own business here!' said Peter. 'A little farmhouse sandwich and cake shop.'

'Peter's right,' said Janet. 'You could set up some tables and chairs outside the kitchen doors on the patio. Oh! And I have the perfect name for what you could call it! Scamper's Kitchen.'

Scamper barked loudly.

'See? Scamper likes it,' said Janet.

'Do you think so?' asked Peter and Janet's mum, getting a bit excited about the idea. 'I do love that name!'

Peter and Janet both nodded enthusiastically.

'Well, I suppose there's no harm in writing "Scamper's Farmhouse Kitchen" on these little paper tags I have here and attaching them to the sandwich orders, is there?' she said, grinning. 'Just so everyone sees where they came from. And who knows what the future holds!'

Peter looked up at the clock. It was past eleven.

'Oh, no,' he said. 'We've done it again!'

Peter and Janet grabbed the plates of food. They were expecting a special guest to join them for their meeting and didn't want to be late!

'Here,' said their mum. 'I made you another small box of Scottish tablet. Don't let Jack eat it all, OK?'

'We won't,' said Janet.

'Thanks, Mum!' called Peter as they both ran out of the door and down to the shed at the bottom of the garden.

'So,' said Mrs Bagnell, sticking her head round the shed door. 'This is the famous secret headquarters. It's very cosy. Am I allowed to come in?'

'Of course,' said Janet. 'Here, you can have my chair. I'll sit on the floor with Scamper.'

'Jam tart?' said Jack, holding out a plate full of delicious-looking tarts. 'The yellow ones are apricot and mango. They're amazing!'

Mrs Bagnell smiled and took one. 'Thank you,' she said. 'Now shall I tell you all why I'm here?'

'Is it about Adaline?' asked George.

'Yes,' said Mrs Bagnell. 'I managed to find her by myself in the theatre after everyone had left. There might be a few extra doors I didn't mention to the police at the time. I wanted to be alone with her to talk. I hoped I could convince her to turn herself in and try to start her life fresh again. And she agreed.'

'That's great news! Thanks so much for coming to let us know,' said Janet.

'Well, that's not the only reason I came,' Mrs Bagnell said, setting her jam tart down for a second. 'I wanted to ask you all how you'd feel about being in another play.'

George gulped.

'At the theatre?' asked Barbara.

'The play was a bit of a disaster,' said Mrs Bagnell. 'And not quite the "grand opening" everyone had hoped for. It didn't even last the full week! So I came up with the idea that we'd put on a free play for the community. But I need your help to make it work. What do you think? Could you bear to go back to the theatre?'

The Seven looked round excitedly.

'Yes!' said Barbara, jumping up. 'We'd love to!'

'That's wonderful news, I'm so pleased! Right,' said Mrs Bagnell, getting up. 'I'd better go. I have a thousand phone calls to make and favours to call in to make this all work.'

'Do you know what the play will be about yet?' asked Janet.

Mrs Bagnell turned and smiled at them. 'Oh, yes,' she said. 'I was up all last night thinking about it. I think I'd like to do a scary one!'

George gulped.

'And I thought I'd call it *The Theatre Ghost*! What do you think?'

Enid Blyton®

THE

SECRET SEVEN

SOLVE THE MYSTERY!

And don't miss . . .

The first Secret Seven mystery by prizewinning author Pamela Butchart!

THE SECRET SEVEN

READ ALL 15 CLASSIC STORIES!

Enid Blyton®

THE
SECRET SEVEN

SOLVE THE MYSTERY!

Solve every puzzle, just like the Secret Seven, in this fun book of 100 tricky codes, puzzles, sudokus, crosswords and more!

Enid Blyton

THE FAMOUS FIVE

Join the Adventure!

Read all 21 classic stories!

© Chris Close

PAMELA BUTCHART

is the bestselling and award-winning author of the Baby Aliens young fiction series, for which she has won the Blue Peter Best Book Award 2015 for *The Spy Who Loved School Dinners* and the Children's Book Award 2016 for *My Head Teacher is a Vampire Rat*. She has also been shortlisted for the Laugh Out Loud Book Award (Lollies) and is one of the fastest growing children's fiction authors in the UK. Pamela wrote a World Book Day book for 2018. She has published two Secret Seven stories: *Mystery of the Skull* and *Mystery of the Theatre Ghost*.

Enid Blyton®

is one of the most popular children's authors of all time. Her books have sold over 500 million copies and have been translated into other languages more often than any other children's author.

Enid Blyton adored writing for children. She wrote over 600 books and hundreds of short stories. *The Famous Five* books, now 75 years old, are her most popular. She is also the author of other favourites including *The Secret Seven*, *The Magic Faraway Tree*, *Malory Towers* and *Noddy*.

Born in London in 1897, Enid lived much of her life in Buckinghamshire and adored dogs, gardening and the countryside. She was very knowledgeable about trees, flowers, birds and animals. Dorset – where some of the Famous Five's adventures are set – was a favourite place of hers too.

Enid Blyton's stories are read and loved by millions of children (and grown-ups) all over the world. Visit enidblyton.co.uk to discover more.